Like a Mighty Stream

Like a Mighty Stream

Trailblazing Women of the Reformation

Sukeshinie Goonatilleke

Copyright © Sukeshinie Goonatilleke 2025

The author assumes full responsibility for the accuracy of all facts and quotations cited in this book.

Bible quotations within the stories are taken from the Holy Bible, King James Version.

Bible quotations elsewhere are taken from the New King James Version®. Copyright © 1982 by Thomas Nelson. Used by permission. All rights reserved.

Proudly published and printed in Australia by
Signs Publishing
Warburton, Victoria.

Edited by Lauren Webb
Proofread by Nathan Brown
Cover design by Shane Winfield
Cover images by istockphoto.com
Typeset in Adobe Caslon Pro 11.5/15 pt

ISBN (print edition) 978 1 923352 20 9
ISBN (ebook edition) 978 1 923352 21 6
ISBN (audiobook edition) 978 1 923352 22 3

For Elyse and Carys

"But let justice run down like water,
And righteousness like a mighty stream."
—Amos 5:24

Contents

Preface ix

1. Margaret Blaurer
   Light Dawning in the Darkness 1

2. Anne of Bohemia and Joan of Kent
   Advocates Before the Throne 13

3. Ursula Cotta
   A Bowl of Grace 22

4. Cornelia Teellinck
   A Confession of Faith 31

5. Marie Dentière
   A Time to Speak 43

6. Jenny Geddes
   Radical Dissent 51

7. Elizabeth Cruciger
   A Song of Solace 58

8. Anna Bullinger
   Love That Suffers Long 67

9. Argula von Grumbach
   The Advocate 77

10. Wibrandis Rosenblatt
    A Light in the Window 85

11. Margaret of Navarre
    A Shelter in the Time of Storm 93

12. Jeanne d'Albret
    Within Gates of Truth 104
13. Margarethe Prüss
    The Little Print Shop at the Wood Market 115
14. Renée of France
    A Place of Greater Safety 122
15. Anne Askew
    The Final Word 132
16. Elizabeth Tyrwhit
    Words of Revival 144
17. Elizabeth Welsh
    The School of Hard Knocks 154
18. Marie Durand, Isabeau Menet and Anne Goutez
    A Bond That Strengthens 163
19. Elizabeth of Denmark
    A Faithful Witness 174
20. Katharina Zell
    A Circle of Refuge 183

Acknowledgments 191
Bibliography 193

Preface

In 1933, German pastor Dietrich Bonhoeffer gave a lecture in which he described the duty of the church as not only "to bandage the wounds of victims beneath the wheels of injustice, but to jam a spoke into the wheel itself."* The brave men and women of the Reformation engaged in this work by choosing to speak against the oppressive regime of the medieval church. Their stories are not simply narratives of courage and commitment; they ring with the determination to stand for liberty and truth.

The themes of the Reformation are more relevant now than they have ever been, and the world needs the gospel more now than it ever has. As Christians, we need to understand the importance of religious liberty, freedom of conscience, and the separation of church and state, and find tangible ways to reach our communities with Jesus' love. This book explores these themes through stories of women whose faith compelled them to action.

The highlight reel of the Reformation has always been dominated by men—a truth that is not limited to this period of history alone. History has traditionally been recorded, recounted and revised by men, for men and about men. But recent decades have brought change as women in academia have risen up to highlight the voices of women who have gone before us. Their stories are vital to our understanding of our past, which in turn shapes both our present and our future.

The 20 short stories in this book present women who were trailblazers in their own right—some were wives and mothers, but they were also writers, poets, social reformers, preachers, teachers and

---

* <https://www.bonhoeffer-initiative.com/en/dietrich-bonhoeffer/bonhoeffers-work>

legislators. Some of them had more agency than others, yet they all worked towards the common goal that Jesus described in Luke 4:18:

> The Spirit of the Lord is upon Me,
> Because He has anointed Me
> To preach the gospel to the poor;
> He has sent Me to heal the broken-hearted,
> To proclaim liberty to the captives
> And recovery of sight to the blind,
> To set at liberty those who are oppressed.

The women in this book were poor, broken-hearted, captive, blind and oppressed until the gospel brought them healing, relief, liberty and hope. In turn, they offered healing, relief, liberty and hope to others in a variety of ways. Marie Dentière was the first woman to preach publicly during the Reformation; Elizabeth Cruciger was the first woman to write Protestant hymns; Jeanne d'Albret was the first Protestant queen in Europe; Margaret Blaurer was the first to establish a relief society for women; and Margaret Prüss was the first female printer of the Reformation. The service of these women was tremendously influential in their communities, nations and the world. Their stories remind us that we too can use the gifts God has given us to impact our communities and contexts.

While I have tried to stay as true to the historical record as possible in telling these stories, I have taken some artistic liberty in filling in the gaps so the narrative flows smoothly. The historical notes at the end of each story give a sense of the facts of each woman's life. The names used in the story titles are the women's married names or the names they are most known by. Where applicable, the women's maiden names are included in the historical notes.

As always, I pray that you are blessed, challenged and inspired by this book in equal measure. Now more than ever, the world needs men and women who are willing to meet the growing tide of hopelessness and oppression with the light of truth—truth that is centred in the person of Jesus and rooted in God's Word.

Preface

Each of these women of the Reformation were committed to this cause, which spurred them forward to "let justice run down like water, and righteousness like a mighty stream" (Amos 5:24).

Sukeshinie (Suki) Goonatilleke

1

Margaret Blaurer

LIGHT DAWNING IN THE DARKNESS

Konstanz, Germany
Summer, 1528

Brothers could be annoying creatures, and Margaret had been blessed with two. One of them sauntered towards her, suspiciously nonchalant, and draped an arm around her shoulder as she kneaded a lump of dough.

"Do you think you have enough food for a visitor?" he asked.

Margaret stopped her kneading to look up at him with a raised brow. "Have you invited someone without asking me and are now trying to ascertain if we will actually be able to feed the man?" she demanded.

Ambrose had the grace to look sheepish as he withdrew his arm and rubbed the back of his neck. "He's a friend, Maggie, and you know we need all the friends we can get right now." He paused, lips pursed as he studied her. "In fact, I think you've heard of him. His name's Martin Bucer—the great reformer from Strasbourg."

Margaret huffed and went back to beating her dough, imagining it was her brother's head. "It won't matter if he's the Apostle Paul if we haven't got enough food to feed him," she muttered, shaking her head. "Aren't Thomas and our cousins coming for dinner? I've only made enough for four grown men."

"But surely it can stretch to accommodate a fifth?" Ambrose cajoled.

Margaret blew out an exasperated sigh, then wiped her sweaty brow with the back of her hand. "You'll just have to eat less," she said sweetly. "And I'm making apple strudel for dessert, which means you'll have to share."

Ambrose grinned, then planted a loud kiss on her cheek. "You're a gem, Maggie, and don't worry. Martin doesn't need any apple strudel. Just bread and cheese will do."

Despite herself, Margaret laughed and shooed him out of the kitchen, shaking her head. Brothers. Despite the irritation they caused, she couldn't really complain about being blessed with two.

Martin Bucer turned out to be as loud and opinionated as her brothers. Their combined verbosity made for lively, if not tranquil, dinner conversation. Ambrose and Thomas, along with their cousins Johannes and Konrad Zwick, were known as the reformers of Konstanz. A year ago, the city had been declared reformist and turned on its head. Churches had been stripped of their icons, monasteries had been shut down and priests had fled. Her brothers had preached the gospel from every available pulpit. Thomas had become mayor of the city and Ambrose was the pastor of the fledgling reformed church.

"And where do you fit into all this, Mistress Blaurer?" Martin asked as he tucked the last bite of stew-soaked bread into his mouth.

Margaret rose to offer him another serving, which he eagerly accepted. "I'm chief housekeeper, cook, laundress and general helper of the reform movement," she said dryly, sawing through the dwindling loaf of bread and handing a slice to their famished guest.

He nodded thoughtfully. "Have you no desire to get married?"

His question set her family to choking, then laughing over their food. Finally, Ambrose spoke, thumping his chest as he gasped for breath. "I can't afford to let Maggie get married," he said, wiping tears of mirth from his eyes. "No-one makes flaky, delectable apple strudel like she does."

Rolling her eyes, Margaret left the table to bring over the dessert in question.

"But marriage is honourable," Martin insisted, watching her intently as she sliced the strudel.

Thomas groaned. "You sound like Wolfgang Capito pontificating on the merits of marriage," he muttered. Capito, a friend and fellow reformer, was notorious for his matchmaking campaigns, and hassled friends and acquaintances alike into surprisingly happy, successful marriages.

"So, you truly do not mean to marry, Mistress Blaurer?" Martin pressed, as Margaret handed him the first slice of strudel with a generous helping of cream.

"You can call me Maggie," she said, turning back to cut a second slice. "And it has not escaped me that you have not asked Ambrose the same question." She smiled sweetly at Martin, who grinned in return.

"Oh, don't worry," he assured her, scooping up a bite of strudel, "I plan to badger your brother eventually, but for now my interest rests entirely on you."

"Thank the Lord for that," Ambrose muttered, digging into his own dessert.

Martin paused a moment to savour another bite of strudel, then turned his attention back to Margaret. "Well?" he asked, raising his eyebrows.

Margaret handed a final helping of strudel to her cousin before turning to serve herself. "No," she said simply, adding a dollop of cream to the plate. "I truly do not mean to marry."

"And why not?" Martin pressed.

"Oh, for heaven's sake, Martin, leave her alone!" Thomas exclaimed, wiping his mouth with the back of his sleeve.

Margaret frowned at him before turning her attention back to Martin. "I don't mind telling you why," she said with a shrug. "I believe God has called me to singleness—and with good reason. Ambrose has the gift of preaching and Thomas has the gift of leadership, but God has given me the gift of ministry to the poor. That is my work.

"Since the city has become reformist, all the monasteries and convents have shut down, and we all know they were the primary source of aid for the poor and sick. They were also where many of the children were sent for an education.

"My brothers and cousins may have introduced the gospel to the city, but the people need more than God's Word to live on. The poor need food, clothes and shelter. Children need an education. With no nuns and monks to provide these things, somebody else must do so."

Margaret paused when she realised that the men had stopped their eating and fallen silent.

"What?" she asked, gazing from one dumbstruck face to another. "I thought the strudel tasted fine?"

Martin cleared his throat, then dug into his strudel with his fork. "Yes," he said, taking a large bite to prove his point, "it's delicious. It's just that I had not thought about all the practical charity that needed to be taken up in the absence of the Roman Church."

Margaret scraped the last crumbs of strudel from her plate, nodding thoughtfully. "Konstanz needs someone to create new institutions for the relief of the poor and for women and children," she said. "And I mean to do that."

A few days later, Margaret hurried to keep up with her brother, who loped ahead of her like a man going to war. "Thomas," she gasped, as she came abreast of him. "What do you think?"

Thomas's stride faltered as he cast a startled glance at Margaret, appearing to only just realise she was walking beside him.

"Well?" she demanded, eyeing her brother, who had now slowed his gait.

"Did you ask me a question?" he queried.

"Oh, for heaven's sake!" Margaret exclaimed. She came to a halt, setting her hands on her hips as she stared her brother down. "I've been nattering in your ear since we left the city council building! Do you mean to tell me you haven't heard a word I've said?"

Thomas sighed and rubbed his forehead. "It's been a long day," he muttered. "I've had to deal with irate townsfolk, disgruntled councillors and fleeing clergy asking for money. You know the city is in upheaval."

"Which is precisely why I came to see you this morning," Margaret countered, refusing to offer him a jot of sympathy.

"Fine," he snapped. He resumed his march down the muddy street and said over his shoulder, "What do you want?"

Gritting her teeth, Margaret scrambled to catch up with him. "I need a building."

Thomas came to an abrupt halt once more, arching a brow as he turned to face her. "A building?" he repeated incredulously.

Margaret nodded. "A building."

"Whatever for?"

"We need an infirmary, Thomas. A place where those too poor to call a doctor can come to be treated. We also need a place for poor children to be educated. And we need a charity house, where we can hand out clothes, food and other necessities." Margaret watched her brother's face, trying to decipher his expression.

"You were serious then, when you told Bucer you wanted to offer relief to the poor in Konstanz."

"I was serious," Margaret agreed with a nod. "We don't have a poor society, and with all the convents and monasteries shutting down, we need a means to provide relief and medical help to the poor."

Thomas ran a hand down his face and Margaret noticed how weary he looked. Sympathy welled in her chest as she realised afresh the magnitude of the task that rested on his shoulders as the mayor of a city racked with conflict and change. She placed a hand on his arm. "I know you are inundated with work," she said, gentling her tone. "But this is just as important as removing icons from churches and ensuring the gospel is preached. We need to show people that the gospel not only ministers to their spiritual needs but to their physical needs as well."

Finally, Thomas nodded. "You can have one of the abandoned convents for the work."

Margaret's eyes widened. "Really?" she breathed.

Thomas grinned. "Really. And let me know what your needs are. I will see what money I can channel to you from the city council funds."

Margaret's face broke into a grin and she squeezed her brother's arm in gratitude. "God bless you, Thomas. That is more than I had hoped for."

Thomas laid his hand over hers and squeezed back. "I am glad to have a worker like you in this city, Maggie," he said softly. "God knows we need your heart and hands and mind to further the work of the gospel here."

With that, he turned and continued down the street. Margaret watched him go, her smile undiminished.

Over the following weeks, Margaret scrubbed and dusted one of the city's abandoned convents with the help of her brothers, cousins and a few women who were eager to embrace her cause. She found bedding, linens and other necessities for both a school and a hospital.

For days on end, she worked from dawn till dusk, dragging herself home only to collapse in a heap at the dinner table. Thomas's wife took pity on them, sending over enough fresh bread, stew and cheese to keep them from starving.

"Do you think you're going to be able to manage the influx of people who will stream through your doors?" Ambrose asked her one night as they sat at the dinner table.

Margaret could barely lift her spoon to her mouth. She shrugged, too weary to answer.

Ambrose eyed her critically. "Maggie, you'll not do anyone any good if you run yourself into the ground," he lectured.

Margaret groaned, dropped her spoon into her bowl and laid her head on the table. "I'm too tired to think, Ambrose," she mumbled. "All I want is to have a hot soak in the tub and go to bed, but I'm too weary to fetch the water or even stand up."

There was a moment of silence, followed by the scrape of wood on wood. Margaret guessed that Ambrose had stood up. She must have drifted off to sleep after that, for the next thing she knew, Ambrose was gently shaking her awake.

"Maggie," he said softly. "Wake up."

Moaning, Margaret lifted her head. She stretched her neck from side to side, trying to ease the stiffness in her muscles. She rose and was beginning to leave the kitchen when she spotted the steaming tub in the corner. Wide-eyed, she turned to Ambrose.

"I drew you a bath," he said with a sheepish smile. "Don't get used to it though." He shuffled out of the kitchen and closed the door behind him.

Margaret grinned. Brothers. She couldn't imagine life without them.

Konstanz, Germany
Summer, 1541

Despite Martin Bucer's best efforts, Margaret had managed to remain unmarried. She enjoyed her simple life—visiting widows and orphans, caring for sick women, teaching children to read. While the men in her life championed the cause of the gospel from the pulpit, Margaret found great purpose in her place among the poor and needy in Konstanz.

"You would do a husband an enormous amount of good," Martin commented during one hurried visit.

Margaret rolled her eyes. He had become a fixture in her life over the past years. "I'm married to Christ," she replied, ladling him another bowl of soup.

"What a Romanist thing to say!" Ambrose exclaimed, dipping his bread in his bowl.

"Hardly," Margaret objected. "I'm not a nun—just a woman who enjoys the blessing of being single. Surely that isn't contrary to Scripture. St Paul wrote about it in one of his epistles."

"Can you name which one?" Martin asked teasingly.

Margaret was contemplating throwing a bit of bread at him when the door burst open, and their cousin John burst in, gasping for air.

Ambrose rose so abruptly that he overturned his stool. "What's happened?" he demanded.

"Plague," John gasped, collapsing onto a stool. "They're preparing to sound the bells right now."

Margaret felt the blood drain from her face.

"Are you certain?" Ambrose demanded.

John nodded. "Several cases have been discovered throughout the day. The physicians are certain."

Martin leapt from his seat, exclaiming that he needed to leave at once. "I cannot afford to bring plague to Strasbourg," he said, hurrying to gather his satchel and his cloak.

Ambrose went to help with his horse while Margaret quickly packed him some bread and cheese. She then placed a bowl of soup and a slice of bread before a grateful John before hurrying to the small chamber in their home that housed her medicinal supplies. She gathered herbs, fresh linens and an assortment of bandages, then went back to the kitchen for a kettle and some pots.

"Where are you going?" Ambrose asked as he strode through the back door.

"I'm going to the charity house," she replied. "We can bring the sick women and children there—those who are too poor to send for the physician."

Ambrose's eyes widened. "Have you gone mad?" he demanded. "The last thing you need is to insert yourself among plague victims."

"And what would you have me do, Ambrose?" Margaret asked, glaring at him. "Stay at home while the people of Konstanz suffer? Is that what Christ would have done?"

Before he could respond, she stormed past him and out the door. She would not stay at home watching like a coward while people died alone without aid. She would roll up her sleeves and do what she could to save them.

The plague spread through the city with the speed of lightning, taking with it a staggering number of men, women and children. Ambrose begged Margaret to let the physicians tend to the sick.

"They have those great, long-beaked masks that prevent them from inhaling the plague. You have nothing to protect yourself with and—" He held up a hand to cut off her weary protest. "In most cases there's nothing anyone can do anyway."

"I can't allow someone to die alone and afraid, Ambrose," she said, burying her face in her hands as she sat before the fireplace. She raised her head to look at him. "If I can offer them some comfort in their last hours, then I must do it."

It seemed to Margaret that over the next few weeks she visited every house in Konstanz. She sat beside dying women, cradled ailing children, and when one small girl could not receive the care she needed in her own home, Margaret bundled her in her arms and brought her to her house. At this juncture, Ambrose, who felt he had spent all the breath in his body protesting over the dangers of his sister's activities, simply went to the kitchen to set a kettle of water to boil to draw a bath for the miserable child.

The plague raged for weeks, until finally, almost imperceptibly, it began to abate. Margaret experienced its diminishing strength as fewer and fewer people succumbed to its ravages. The little girl she had brought home recovered and was duly sent back to her relieved parents. The sick-beds in the convent began to empty. Margaret was summoned less frequently from her bed in the middle of the night, until one day she was not summoned at all.

"I think we're over the worst of it," Thomas said, as he strode in unannounced to check on his beleaguered siblings.

Margaret nodded. She rose from her place at the kitchen table, thinking to offer him some refreshment, when a wave of dizziness overtook her. She stumbled, nearly tripping over the bench she had been seated on.

"Maggie?" Thomas cried in alarm, rushing to her side.

"I'm fine," she said weakly. "Just a little . . ." Margaret felt herself sway, heard her brothers' voices in the distance, and then all at once she felt herself engulfed in terrible darkness.

When Margaret awoke, she was tucked snugly in bed beneath her own warm blankets, a fire blazing in the hearth to chase away the chill in her bones. Her throat felt parched, her head pounded, and her eyes felt raw and bruised. Worst of all were the racking chills that washed over her, causing her to shiver and swelter by turns. She heard the door creak open and soft footsteps approach her bed.

"Maggie?" Ambrose whispered.

Margaret moaned, placing a hand to her fevered brow. "Water," she rasped.

Ambrose appeared above her with a cup of water. Gently, he placed his hand beneath her shoulders, lifted her up and dribbled a small trickle of water into her mouth.

"Thank you," she gasped.

A moment later, a cool cloth fell across her forehead, making her sigh with relief. Margaret didn't know how long she remained abed, but every time she awoke, one of her brothers sat beside her, offering her water or a cool cloth, or reading her a letter from one of their many friends. Martin wrote to tell her that he expected her to recover for he could not bear the thought of losing such a good sparring partner.

Yet, despite her most valiant efforts, Margaret felt her strength ebbing with each passing day. One evening, she awoke with a start to Ambrose's soft voice praying over her.

"Oh, God, heal our Maggie," he prayed, his voice breaking. "How can we bear to live without her?"

Margaret felt the hot prick of tears burning her eyes. Quietly, she reached out to clasp his hand. His voice faltered, then rallied, becoming more fervent as he squeezed her hand reassuringly. Margaret silently added her own supplications to his, praying to God for comfort and hope, but above all for the grace to surrender to his will.

When Ambrose finished his prayer, he settled back in his chair to keep vigil beside her bed. Margaret felt the ghost of a smile grace her lips. Brothers. How could she have survived without them?

Margaret Blaurer was born around 1494. Her brother Ambrose Blaurer, a former priest, was known as the Reformer of Konstanz and Württemberg. He, his brother Thomas and cousins John and Conrad Zwick were the nucleus of the reformist movement in Konstanz. In 1527, Konstanz officially declared itself a reformed city. Margaret is credited with establishing the first Protestant women's society to care for the sick, a necessary service following the dismantling of convents. She also cared for the poor and needy and provided children with an education. Margaret was an avid reader who understood the theological nuances of her day, and she had a lively friendship with reformer Martin Bucer, which was mostly conducted via correspondence. Bucer constantly encouraged her to marry and she cheerfully resisted all his efforts. In late 1541, the plague swept through Konstanz. At great personal risk, Margaret cared for the sick, visiting them in their homes to offer assistance and comfort, and subsequently fell ill herself. Ambrose wrote to Martin Bucer, pleading with him to pray for Margaret, who he called "our only comfort." Despite his earnest prayers, Margaret died on November 15, 1541.

2

Anne of Bohemia and Joan of Kent

ADVOCATES BEFORE THE THRONE

Lutterworth, Leicestershire, England
February, 1382

When the summons arrived, John Wycliffe was writing at his desk. He hated interruptions, but the loud pounding was incessant, as was the voice shouting at him to open his door in the name of the king.

"I'm coming, I'm coming," he shouted as he shuffled towards the door. When he opened it, a liveried servant stood before him, holding a sealed parchment. The servant handed it to Wycliffe, who examined the seal, then glanced at the man's livery.

"And who might you be?" Wycliffe asked. He was getting too old to remember which heraldic emblems belonged to which lord, lady, knight or bishop. Too much flora and fauna for his liking.

"I'm a groom in the household of His Grace the Archbishop of Canterbury," the man said, affronted.

Wycliffe grunted, cracking open the shiny wax seal and unfolding the letter. "His Grace the Archbishop of Canterbury, eh?" He paused to eye the man before him once more. "His Grace would do well to remember that his master Jesus Christ did not assume lordly titles while He was on earth. He was a servant who washed His disciples' feet." Wycliffe looked down at the letter. "Perhaps the archbishop serves a master other than Christ."

The man gasped, sputtered, then said, "I had heard of your insolence, sir, but I now see I was not told the half of it."

Wycliffe chuckled as he thrust the missive back at the man. "No, indeed you weren't, for if you've taken offense at what I've just said, you would faint dead away were you to sit through one of my sermons."

When the man made no move to retrieve the proffered letter, Wycliffe waved it about. "Go on then," he said. "Take it and be on your way."

"You have been summoned to appear before the archbishop and others of the king's council to answer to charges of heresy." The man grabbed the parchment and jabbed a finger at it. "You have been accused of 24 counts of heresy, sir. It is no small matter."

Wycliffe waved a dismissive hand. "Rubbish. They accuse me of heresy when all I have done is preach God's Word. Be off with you. Tell them I'm too busy doing God's work in Lutterworth to attend to their foolishness."

With that he shut the door in the slack-jawed groom's face.

Windsor Castle, England
May, 1382

The Queen of England was in her presence chamber sewing shirts with her ladies when the door burst open to admit her mother-in-law. Anne immediately stood and curtsied to the woman who was as intimidating as she was alluring.

"Your Highness," Anne said softly, dipping her head as far as she dared without upsetting her conical headdress. Her mother-in-law,

Joan, dowager Princess of Wales, returned the curtsey but not the greeting.

"I wish to speak to you, child," she said instead. With a flick of her wrist, she dismissed Anne's ladies, who scuttled from the room without a murmur of dissent.

Anne watched them go, tempted to roll her eyes. Her mother-in-law was much like her own mother, the Holy Roman Empress—a formidable, irrepressible force of nature.

When the room was empty save the two of them, Joan eyed her. Though inwardly quaking, Anne held herself very still, unwaveringly returning her mother-in-law's gaze. She had been Queen of England for four of the five months she had lived in this kingdom. Her husband Richard doted on her and she returned his devotion. Everyone thought they were lovesick fools but neither of them cared.

Anne found that her adopted countrymen regarded her with caution, perhaps even suspicion. She supposed it was inevitable given that she could speak no English and had brought no dowry. Yet her husband's adoration more than made up for the chilly English welcome. Anne hoped that the English would come to love her—or at least grow fond of her in time.

Her mother-in-law was like Anne's newly acquired subjects. She didn't hate Anne but she didn't love her either. Richard assured her that his mother's affections would thaw.

"It's hard for her," he had explained when Anne had timidly inquired about his mother. "She was going to be Queen of England, but my father succumbed to his illness, leaving her the dowager Princess of Wales. The crown passed directly to me when my grandfather died. Now you are Queen of England, and she is . . . not."

"Listen carefully for I shall not repeat myself." Joan's voice jolted Anne back to the present. "The king's council has summoned John Wycliffe to appear before them. He has been charged with 24 counts of heresy."

It took a moment for Anne to comprehend the words, but when she did her eyes widened. "Master Wycliffe?"

"They have drawn up a document denouncing him, calling for swift and unyielding punishment."

"Why?" Anne breathed.

Joan clucked her impatience. "Do you not know who John Wycliffe is?" she demanded.

"I do," Anne replied. "I have read his work and I . . . I believe in much of what he preaches and teaches."

Joan's eyes gleamed and she nodded approvingly. "Good. I suspected as much. I have noticed you reading your Bible in Czech every morning, and I surmised that a young woman who reads Scripture in her own language could very well be Wycliffe's disciple."

Anne frowned. "Why would you think that?"

"Because Wycliffe is a firm believer in personal Bible study," Joan smiled slyly, "and I have heard rumours that your countryman Matthias Janovius harboured beliefs similar to Wycliffe's."

Anne's mind whirled, as memories flooded its recesses. Matthias Janovius had been her father's chaplain. Like Wycliffe, he had denounced the mass, insisting that Christ did not inhabit the bread or the wine. Like Wycliffe, he had denounced the abuses of the church, calling for reform. His followers had been persecuted by Anne's father, the Holy Roman Emperor, and Janovius had been banished from Bohemia.

"What will they do to Master Wycliffe?" Anne asked. "Will they banish him like my father banished Janovius?"

Joan laughed. "Hardly. The English Church is too bloodthirsty for that. I imagine they will call for his burning or, at the very least, his imprisonment."

"But he is an old man!" Anne protested, her heart squeezing with compassion and dread.

"They don't care about his age, my dear," Joan said airily. "They only care about the trouble he's causing and, as you well know, he is causing enough to call down a firestorm on the English Church."

Anne thought about this. "Can they threaten him into silence?"

Joan laughed again. "Oh, Anne, if they could have done that, he would have been silenced a long time ago. No, he will not be cowed. Nor will he even bother to appear before them, I suspect."

Anne bit her lip. "Why are you telling me this?"

"Because I have a plan," Joan said with a smile, "and I need an ally."

The Palace of Westminster, London, England
May 21, 1382

Anne hurried to match her mother-in-law's clipped pace as they navigated the labyrinthine galleries of Westminster Palace.

"Do you remember what to do?" Joan asked, eyes forward, face impassive, as they approached the king's presence chamber.

The king was meeting with his advisors at the palace just as John Wycliffe was due to appear before the archbishop's synod at Lambeth Palace, just down the river.

"I remember," Anne murmured, drawing in a deep breath as they paused before the large double doors.

Joan flung the doors open with a flourish, momentarily disrupting the activity within. King Richard looked up, startled, then rose to greet them.

"Lady Mother," he said. "And my beloved. I thought you had gone hawking. Have you already been?" His eyes traced Anne's face, trying to decipher the cause of the unexpected interruption.

"No," Joan said, reclaiming his attention. "We have come to seek the king's favour in a matter of utmost importance."

Everyone in the room froze, watching the dowager Princess of Wales.

Richard frowned. "What matter?" he asked, his eyes darting to Anne. "And what does my wife have to do with this?"

"We have come to intercede on behalf of John Wycliffe," Joan said placidly.

"What?" Richard bellowed, pacing away from them in agitation. He whirled back, pointing a trembling finger at his mother. "Have you lost your mind? You *must* have lost your mind to pursue this matter—and to bring my innocent wife into it!"

Joan was silent for a moment, then said earnestly, "Richard, they plan to condemn him as a heretic."

Richard paced, as agitated as a caged tiger. "What do I care if they condemn him? I have no love for a Lollard—and worse yet, the very fountainhead of all Lollardy."

Anne's heart squeezed. "But he's an innocent old man," she blurted out. "All he has done is uplift the Scriptures. How can he be burned for that?"

Richard gazed at her sharply, his expression warring between disbelief and irritation.

"What you fail to understand," a voice said, "is that Wycliffe's teachings are deceptive and insidious."

Anne turned to face Richard's uncle, John, the Duke of Lancaster.

"There was a time when you were one of his staunchest supporters," Joan said softly.

John scoffed. "Until I realised that he was preaching against the mass, the authority of the pope and nearly every sacrament."

"He is a man who speaks truth," Joan countered. "Are we going to punish him for it?"

"Are you even listening to yourself, Mother?" Richard barked. "He's a man who speaks contrary to the church and that is the end of the matter. The church is the arbiter of truth, not John Wycliffe."

"Yet, Wycliffe says Scripture is the arbiter of all truth. How can anyone disagree with that?" Anne implored.

"He's a heretic," Richard insisted mulishly, glaring at his wife.

"One who must face the consequences of his actions," his uncle agreed.

Tears welled in Anne's eyes, and she fell on her knees before her husband. "Please, my lord," she begged, "spare his life. He has done nothing to deserve death."

"Oh, for heaven's sake!" Richard cried. "He's not even here in London. He doesn't care about the proceedings. Why should any of us?"

"But can they not condemn him in absentia?" Joan asked. "Can they not have him arrested and thrown in prison?"

The room was silent, the tension crackling like a living thing.

"Mercy, my lords," Anne pleaded. "Have mercy."

Lutterworth, Leicestershire, England
June, 1382

John Wycliffe was weary of uninvited guests. Another spate of knocking summoned him from his writing, and when he opened the door, he found himself face to face with yet another sour-faced liveried groom.

"Master John Wycliffe?" the man queried.

Wycliffe eyed him, then nodded. "That's my name," he said. "And who might you be?"

"A messenger from the royal household," the man announced, extending a letter to him.

Wycliffe took it, paused, then glanced up at the man. "Have you come to arrest me, then?" he demanded.

The man's lips twitched, but he shook his head. "No, sir. Last I heard, there was talk of pardoning you. I expect that is what the letter is about."

"Pardoning me, eh?" Wycliffe muttered, slitting open the letter and reading its contents. "It says here they have denounced my teachings—all of them. But they have chosen to refrain from taking any action against me."

The messenger leaned in to whisper conspiratorially, "I was in the king's presence chamber at Westminster Palace, sir, when the council was discussing your matter. The king's mother came in, followed by the queen, and it was those two great ladies who pleaded on your behalf."

Wycliffe gaped at him. "Are you playing me false?"

"Never, sir. It's the whole truth. I was then sent to Lambeth Palace with instructions from the king telling the archbishop to show you clemency. Said they could condemn your writings but that no harm was to come to your person, sir. It was the queen's doing. I saw her on her knees pleading for you, just as she pleaded for those rebellious peasants. And you know how the king can't bear to deny her anything."

"King Richard isn't particularly fond of me," Wycliffe said thoughtfully.

"No, sir, not many people in the church are, but the queen has taken a shine to you." The man lowered his voice even more. "I heard that she's read your work."

Wycliffe's eyes widened in surprise. "Has she, now?" he asked, beaming with pleasure.

The man nodded, as solemn as a tax collector come to receive his dues.

"Well, lad, since you bring good news, would you like to come in for some refreshment? Maybe a bite to eat?"

The man hesitated, then stepped into the house. Wycliffe clapped him on the shoulder as he led him inside. "Now, are you familiar with my teachings at all? Being in the king's household, you must have heard something, surely."

The man nodded. "I am somewhat acquainted with your work, sir, but hardly enough to be conversant."

"And what's your name, lad?"

"Holborn, sir."

Wycliffe slung his arm around Holborn's shoulder. "Well, Holborn, step into my parlour and I shall make you conversant before day's end."

Anne of Bohemia, Queen of England, was born in Prague around 1367 to the Holy Roman Emperor Charles IV and his fourth wife, Elizabeth of Pomerania. During this time, a strong reformatory movement in Bohemia mirrored John Wycliffe's work in England. Anne was likely influenced by the Bohemian reformers John Melice, Conrad Strickna and Matthias Janovius. She is said to have owned personal copies of the Bible in at least three languages and to have read the Bible daily.

Joan of Kent married Edward, the Black Prince, in 1361 and became the first Princess of Wales. They had two sons—Edward of Angoûleme, who died at the age of five, and Richard of Bordeaux, who went on to be King of England.

The two women are significant for their advocacy on behalf of those facing religious persecution. Joan of Kent defended Wycliffe on more than one occasion and, together with Anne of Bohemia, was successful in saving him from serious punishment.

3

Ursula Cotta

A Bowl of Grace

Eisenach, Germany
Winter, 1498

Martin Luther's day had begun with little promise and was ending with even less hope. Not only had he and his companion been forced to spend hours outside being blasted by an icy north wind, but it also seemed they were destined to go home with empty bellies. Again.

"Come on," Gunther urged. "If we don't move, we'll freeze to death."

For a moment, Martin wished that he *could* simply freeze to death, but the prospect of what waited beyond the grave terrified him so thoroughly that he decided he would rather face the miserable prospect of his life. "Let's go back," he said to Gunther, his numb tongue barely forming the words.

"What?" Gunther looked at him as though he had lost his mind. "And go to bed hungry again?"

Martin sighed. Gunther was right. This would be the third night in a row that they would be going to bed hungry if they couldn't scrounge up some food soon. "Well, we've had no success all day." Suddenly, he was angry. "If we go home, we'll be hungry, but at least we won't be so cold. It's not as though the heavens are about to open and rain bread upon us."

At that moment, a single crystalline snowflake fluttered onto his cheek, followed by another, then another. Soon it was snowing steadily. Martin groaned, covering his face with his hands. He dared a glance at Gunther, whose gaze was fixed upon the glowing lights of a house across the whitewashed expanse of St George Square.

"Well?" Martin prompted, half hoping Gunther would simply give up and half hoping he would not.

Gunther let out an exasperated grunt, then he reached out a bony hand, latched on to Martin's thin cloak and began to drag him across the square towards the house.

Ursula had forgotten why she had come upstairs. She was sure it was an important errand that had brought her here, but somehow, when she had seen the two boys standing upon the stoop of the house across the square, the urgent task had faded from her mind. Instead, she had stood at the window transfixed with horror and compassion as she watched the scene before her.

From this distance, she couldn't distinguish their features. All she knew was that they were two male children, dressed completely inadequately for the frigid weather. She had watched them knock on the door and speak a few words to the servant who answered. Then the servant had abruptly swung his long-handled broom at their heads, and the boys had jumped off the stoop like actors in a comedic masque. They had then made their way to another house, only for a matronly servant to plant her fists on her ample hips and begin to lecture them.

Ursula had a vague sense of passing time, but she could not pry herself away from the window. She watched the boys trundle from one home to the next, receiving the same appalling treatment. She wondered who they could be and why they were subjecting themselves to such treatment. And then it came to her—they were charity scholars from St George's School. She supposed she would recognise them if she got a better look at their faces for she saw the boys lining up at the front of the cathedral every Sunday when she went for mass. She knew little about them or their circumstances. She only knew what everyone in Eisenach knew—that some of the boys who attended the school could not afford to pay the full cost of their education. To defray expenses, they were expected to beg for food. However, since the school frowned upon begging outright, the boys were meant to sing for their supper. Many of the residents of the town regarded them as pests—like rats rummaging in the rubbish.

When it began to snow, Ursula bit her lip and shook her head. Perhaps she could . . . And then she saw one of the boys grab hold of the other and haul him with grim determination in the direction her house. Smiling, Ursula turned on her heel and hurried downstairs.

The hollow clang of the brass knocker sounded like a death knell in Martin's mind.

"Smile," Gunther commanded through gritted teeth.

Martin glared at him, then pasted a wide, false smile on his face.

"One, two, three," Gunther counted, and they broke out in a little ditty with practised synchronicity. Heaven knew they had repeated this ritual often enough for it to be second nature.

The rattling of the lock turning caused Martin's entire body to tense. He leaned back, his legs prepared to spring into action should the need arise. The door swung inwards, and Martin's voice faltered, then ground to a halt, as he gaped in wonder at the delicate face framed in the doorway before him. He blinked, opened his mouth, then grunted as Gunther's pointy elbow jabbed into his side. Shooting Gunther a glare, he resumed his singing with as much dignity as a wet, starving 14-year-old boy could muster.

The young woman, who was clearly the lady of the house, waited patiently while they finished their song. Martin thought, distractedly, that she looked familiar. She was most likely a regular parishioner at the cathedral, though he didn't know her name. When they were done, Gunther stepped forward cautiously, holding out his stained sack. "Please, my lady," he began, "may we have some supper?"

They waited, uncertain what to expect from this smiling, pleasant-faced woman. And then she did the most unexpected thing. She extended a slender, astonishingly clean hand towards them saying, "Please come inside!"

For a moment, they regarded her with slack-jawed disbelief. Then they glanced at each other. Gunther tilted his chin up as if to ask, *Well?* To which Martin responded with a shrug—*Why not?* Gunther reciprocated with a shrug of his own, nodded and stepped past Martin into the warm, luxurious interior of the house.

Ursula had minimal experience with adolescent boys—she knew little about their habits and even less about their minds—yet as the two boys stepped into her home, they felt strangely familiar. One of them—the one who had stopped singing abruptly when she had opened the door—shuddered involuntarily, his wide, limpid eyes taking in the opulence around him. He then sniffed, rubbing his threadbare sleeve beneath his nose. Ursula cringed, then straightened her shoulders, determined to make them feel welcome.

"And what are your names?" she asked cheerfully.

"Gunther," one of them said, shifting uncertainly from foot to foot.

"Martin Luther," said the other, tightening his arms across his bony frame.

Both boys were thin, their gaunt faces making their eyes look impossibly large and their cheekbones like blades. The one who had identified himself as Martin had grimy hair that stuck up stiffly from his head in spiky tufts.

Like A Mighty Stream

More porcupine than boy, Ursula mused to herself, caught between amusement and pity.

"Well, Gunther and Martin," she said, smiling. "Welcome to my home. I am Mistress Ursula Cotta."

A stunned footman hovered in the background, and Ursula gestured for him to take the boys' cloaks. He hesitated, then took the filthy garments with a look of such disdain that Ursula glared her displeasure. She wondered if she should ask him to burn them, but then realised she had nothing to replace them with, so she merely nodded before turning to lead the way towards the kitchen.

"Now, let's see what we can find for you to eat."

If heaven ever opened to welcome a poor ingrate like him, Martin imagined it would closely resemble Ursula Cotta's kitchen. It was large, warm and filled with the delicious scents of food. So much food. He glanced at Gunther, who was staring at the commotion before him with glazed eyes.

Ursula sat them at a rough-hewn table, where they watched the cooks and maids engaged in their practised dance of supper preparation. Ursula served the boys herself, placing a platter of fresh yeasty bread before them, followed by cheese, dried fruit, bowls of steaming stew and finally a warm mug filled with a seething spicy drink.

Suddenly, Martin felt the sharp sting of tears in his eyes. He swallowed and blinked, desperately trying to swipe at his eyes before Gunther noticed, but it was all in vain. Before he could even fathom what was happening, he was hunched over the table sobbing like a fool, right into the platter of bread.

Gunther turned to him, frozen in shock, while Ursula uttered a distressed little cry as she situated herself beside him.

"Oh, don't cry," she said softly, her hands fluttering around him like a butterfly uncertain where to land. She finally placed them in her lap, where she wrung them together until her fingers whitened with the strain. Finally, she spoke, "How is it you came to be a charity scholar, Martin?"

Martin hesitated, expelled a shuddering breath, then looked up. Gunther was watching him, his expression a mixture of impatience and compassion. Martin gestured to the food before them. "May we eat, my lady?" he asked, his voice thick with suppressed tears.

"Oh!" Ursula exclaimed, as though only just remembering the feast before them. "Yes, please." She gestured for them to begin and neither boy needed to be told twice.

In between bites of food, Martin divulged the story of his life—his close-knit family, his father's desperate bid to carve out a living from the few mines he had managed to purchase. "His income is insufficient to pay for all my expenses at school," Martin admitted, "but he wants me to become a lawyer." He hesitated, then continued, telling her of the previous school he had attended, of the dreadful beatings handed down by surly monks. "And then my father sent me here to Eisenach," he concluded. "We have relatives in the area, you see, and he thought they might shelter me."

Ursula regarded him thoughtfully. "And your relatives could not help?"

Martin shrugged, squirming. "I don't think they had the means to provide for another mouth."

Ursula stood abruptly and gave them both a brief nod, before walking purposefully from the room.

Ursula prided herself on her ability to persuade her husband to do whatever she asked of him, but she was suddenly doubting that skill. Watching Conrad, who regarded her with a mixture of incredulity and exasperation, she couldn't tell if he would agree to her scheme or not.

"We can't possibly," he finally declared.

"But we must," she insisted, holding his gaze steadily.

Conrad sighed, rubbing a hand down his face. "Are you sure he is a Luther?" he asked again.

"From Mansfield," she confirmed.

He turned away from her, hands clasped behind his back as he paced before the roaring fireplace. She allowed him a moment to consider, to weigh all his options. Conrad was a cautious man, and Ursula knew she was asking him to take an enormous risk. Would he? It seemed unlikely. Yet how could he not? When he turned to face her, she saw wariness in his eyes and her heart sank.

"Oh, please, Conrad," she begged. She rushed forward to clasp his hands in hers. "I feel as though God has sent him to us and we cannot turn him away—especially knowing who he is." A Luther from Mansfield. Distant cousin to Conrad. That emaciated little porcupine man-child in their kitchen was a member of their extended family, and he so desperately needed their help. Help they could easily provide.

Conrad groaned, then heaved a sigh. "You will not relent, will you?"

Ursula offered him a tentative smile. "At least come and meet him," she said, dragging him towards the door.

When they reached the kitchen, all activity ceased. The servants stared as the master of house strode into their domain. Conrad came to a halt before a stunned Martin, who seemed to shrink beneath the weight of his gaze. Ursula bit her lip, willing her husband to soften his grim expression.

"I hear you have come to us in search of a meal," Conrad began, lowering himself to sit on the bench across from the white-faced boys.

Ursula discreetly shooed the servants back to work, then hovered nervously behind her husband as he questioned Martin. For his part, Martin answered clearly, concisely and respectfully, immediately endearing himself to Conrad, who considered him with growing admiration. When Martin ceased speaking, silence hung thick around them.

Then Conrad cleared his throat. "Well, Martin, how would you like to come and live in our house?"

Weeks later, lying on his soft down bed, staring at the silken canopy above him, Martin could hardly believe his fortune. He had come to this home seeking nothing more than a crust of bread, yet here he was, happily situated within its walls as a permanent resident. He was so comfortable, so well fed and clothed that he hardly recognised himself. The most important change in his circumstances was his ability to finally concentrate on his education. The impossible dream of going to university now seemed nearer than it had ever been. In fact, his father had written to tell him that he was saving money to send him to the University of Erfurt. It was all too good to be true.

Sighing, Martin shut his eyes. He had always believed that God was angry with him, but now he wondered if that was true. Perhaps God was not the tyrant he had believed Him to be. Perhaps God was a little like Conrad and Ursula—or perhaps they were like God. Perhaps, beyond belief, God was kind, generous and even merciful.

Ursula Cotta (née Schalb) was the wife Conrad Cotta, mayor of Eisenach, where Martin Luther attended St George's Latin School in his teens. He was taken on as a charity scholar—an arrangement that required him to beg for food. While begging one day, likely in January or February of 1498, he met Ursula Cotta. His reception at the Cotta home was different to anything he had experienced before. After feeding him, the Cottas took him in as their ward. He lived with them for three years, until he enrolled at the University of Erfurt in 1501. Years later, after he had set the Reformation in motion, he mentioned the Cottas in a sermon, and they even visited him to listen to his preaching on occasion. Ursula Cotta's hospitality gave Martin Luther a glimpse of the character of God, and he was always grateful for that.

4

Cornelia Teellinck

A Confession of Faith

Middelburg, Zeeland, The Low Countries
Summer, 1566

Cornelia was only 12 when her world turned upside down. Standing beneath the summer sun, in an open field in Middelburg, she watched the crowds surge around her. She stayed close to her sister Susanna, keeping a sharp eye out for their brother Joos, whom they had lost in the crowd as soon as they arrived.

"Can you see him?" Susanna asked, reaching out to hold Cornelia's hand.

Cornelia stood on tiptoe and craned her neck, but it was useless. She was too short to see over the towering farmers who moved before her like thick-shouldered trees. She shook her head, then yelped when someone stepped on her bare foot.

"I told you to wear your shoes," Susanna muttered, yanking her away from the offender, who mumbled a hasty apology before ambling off.

"It's too hot for shoes," Cornelia whined, tugging at the cap on her head that made her scalp prickle with heat.

Susanna slapped her hand away. "Stop it! You'll not discard your cap in public."

Sighing, Cornelia dropped her hand, then pouted up at her sister. "Why did you bring me?"

Susanna rolled her eyes in irritation. "We couldn't very well leave you home alone, could we?"

Cornelia studied her sulkily. Susanna was 15 and Joos had just turned 18. Their parents had died within four years of each other, leaving them orphaned. Thankfully, Joos had been old enough to assume guardianship over his sisters after their father died. He had left them a large home and a handsome inheritance, allowing them the luxury of a comfortable living. But Cornelia knew they would all relinquish the wealth in a heartbeat if they could have their parents back.

"There!" Susanna suddenly exclaimed, rising on her toes to peer across the crowd. She raised her hand over her head, waving frantically. "Joos!" she shouted. "Here!"

Their brother appeared beside them a few moments later, his brow crinkled in an irritated frown. "You could have just waved," he grumbled, scrubbing a hand through his hair as he glanced surreptitiously about. "You didn't have to bellow like that."

Susanna clucked her tongue. "As if you would have seen me waving through this crowd of people."

Joos's eyes dipped towards Cornelia, then travelled down to her bare feet. His frown deepened. "Where on earth are your shoes?"

Cornelia opened her mouth to defend herself but a man's voice interrupted her. He called out to the crowd from atop a wagon on the far side of the field, directing everyone to sit down on the grass. Joos grabbed Cornelia's hand, then dipped his head at Susanna, motioning her to follow. He quickly wove his way through the crowd until they reached a tree. He hefted Cornelia onto one of the low hanging branches and she wrapped an arm around the trunk to steady herself. Susanna leaned against the thick trunk beside Joos. The man was speaking again, introducing the preacher for the day.

"Who is he?" Susanna asked, as the young preacher stepped up onto the wagon, which acted as a makeshift stage.

"Cornille de la Zenne," Joos said, as the man lifted his arms, urging the crowd to be silent. "He is the son of a blacksmith from Roubaix. He preached in Tournai some weeks ago to a crowd of about 4000."

"Why has he come here?" Susanna asked.

Joos shrugged. "He goes where the people will hear him."

Cornille de la Zenne called for the congregation to bow their heads. Cornelia shut her eyes but peeked through her lashes, observing his bowed head and fervent expression as he prayed. This was the beginning of trouble in these parts, she was sure of it. She had already heard, by eavesdropping on her overbearing siblings while they whispered to each other at night, that reformist preachers were sweeping across the Low Countries, preaching the gospel in open fields to anyone willing to hear. It was a revolution, Joos had said, not only against the Roman Church but also against their Spanish overlords.

"Let the King of Spain try to stop us now," Joos had whispered to Susanna, his face triumphant. "We are as unstoppable as Luther was before the emperor at the Diet of Worms."

Cornelia had read about the Diet of Worms. She had read a great deal in fact, about all sorts of things because her father believed in educating his daughters as well as he educated his only son. Yet, her father had died a firm Romanist, receiving extreme unction at the hands of the local priest. What would he think if he knew his three children had flocked to hear a hedge preacher in Middelburg speaking against the church from Scripture? Cornelia knew he would have been appalled, but she wondered if he would have stopped them.

Cornille finished his prayer, then reaching into the pocket of his leather vest, he pulled out a small object. Cornelia squinted, trying to determine what it was. Cornille held it triumphantly over his head and cried, "This, my brothers and sisters, is the living Word of God! It is all you need for doctrine, for reproof, for instruction in righteousness! It is all you need to determine what is truth!"

A murmur rippled across the crowd as Cornille opened the small Bible and began to read. "In his second letter to the Corinthians, the

Apostle Paul writes, 'If any man be in Christ, he is a new creature: old things are passed away; behold, all things are become new!'" He paused. "I declare to you this day, beloved, that all you need for salvation is Christ Jesus our Lord. Not the rituals or mummery of the church, not the incantations of the priests. For in the epistle to the Romans we are told, 'The just shall live by faith.' Faith in what? I will tell you—faith in the shed blood of Christ, who is able not only to atone for our sins but also to cleanse us from all our unrighteousness. Look to Christ. He is our rock, our only hope of salvation."

Cornelia's arm tightened around the tree trunk as her heart beat wildly in her chest. All her life she had learned that salvation could be obtained through the sacraments of the church. It was like buying a piece of fabric from a merchant. If she would produce the necessary currency of good works, God would dispense a measure of grace proportionate to what she had paid. But as she sat listening to Cornille de la Zenne, she felt a pinprick of heat in her chest. It grew and expanded, filling her with so many emotions—peace, joy, hope—until she thought she might burst from the fullness of it all.

Beside her, she heard Joos expel a sharp breath. Beneath her, Susanna lifted a trembling hand to her lips. Cornelia felt the beginnings of a smile tugging at her lips. They would be leaving this field in Middelburg with an entirely different kind of faith.

Zierikzee, Zeeland, The Low Countries
Summer, 1570

Cornelia watched the ships bobbing like toy sailboats upon the azure waters of the distant bay. The wind washed over her, cool and refreshing, as the sun began to dip below the horizon. Since the day she heard Cornille de la Zenne preach the gospel, she had been relentless in her pursuit of the truth. It was like a fire, liquefying her bones, searing her heart, threatening to consume her. She could hardly imagine who or what she would have become had it not been for that life-changing moment that tethered her to Christ like a ship anchored at port. It was the inferno of her faith that had brought her here, to this place, to think, to pray, to seek God's guidance.

She hadn't yet said anything to Susanna or Joos, though she knew she would have to divulge her secrets to them eventually. First, she needed to be certain of her course. Cornelia closed her eyes and turned her face to the sky, sending her pleas for clarity heavenward as she savoured the caress of the wind on her cheeks. She was fervently petitioning God when a loud gasp floated up to her, followed by Susanna's voice.

"Cornelia Teellinck! You get down from there right this minute!"

Dropping her faced into her hands, Cornelia groaned. "Susanna—" she began, but her sister was already screaming for their brother.

"Joos! Joos!" Her shrill voice was loud enough to bring the neighbours running. "She is up on the roof again! I fear she will fall and break her neck and then what will we do?"

Sighing in resignation, Cornelia lowered herself slowly onto her back, gazing up at the beribboned sky awash with the pale pinks and gauzy purples of encroaching twilight. She heard the tell-tale scrape of a boot on the window ledge, then a grunt, and finally she felt the warm weight of her brother's long body as he settled himself beside her.

"Well, at least we know you haven't run off to join a travelling company of players," he said mildly.

Cornelia turned her face towards him and found him smiling at her. They stared at one another for a beat before bursting into synchronised laughter. Groaning, Cornelia covered her face with her hands. "I just wanted a moment's peace," she moaned.

"Susanna wanted to ask you about the dressmaker's appointment tomorrow," Joos said, his voice holding a hint of rebuke. "Imagine her surprise when she came into your room to find you missing and your window wide open."

"Am I awful?" she asked, uncovering her face.

Joos's profile remained solemn, though Cornelia detected a faint twitch of his lips as he shrugged. "Susanna worries that you will not turn into a proper lady," he said, casting a sideways glance at her.

Cornelia said nothing. "She loves you very much, Corrie. You know that," Joos said softly. "She bears a great weight of responsibility where you are concerned."

Cornelia knew this and she loved her sister for it, but her motherly concern still chafed. "I am not deliberately trying to rile her."

"No," Joos agreed, "but you manage to do it with such frequency that I wonder if you secretly relish it."

Cornelia waved a hand before her face, choosing to ignore his sly jibe. "I came to think. I needed . . . air, not walls around me as I did so."

Joos rose to a seated position, drawing his knees to his chest as he gazed out into the distance. Cornelia did the same, tucking her skirts around her knees as she waited for him to speak.

"Is this about what happened at the services this week?" he finally asked.

"Were you not affected by the arrests, Joos? Do you not feel that we are vulnerable and terribly fragmented? There is not a day that goes by when I do not wonder when we shall be discovered."

"It is the lot of every Protestant in the Low Countries at present," he said matter-of-factly.

"And then I wonder, when men like Rochus or Couwenberch are arrested, what will happen to the flocks they were shepherding? Do our people even know what they believe?"

"If they didn't, they certainly wouldn't risk life and limb to practise it," Joos pointed out.

Cornelia huffed out a breath. "Sometimes I think that reformists in Zeeland need . . . something to bind us together. To give us clarity and purpose regardless of what might happen to the leaders in our midst."

"Our leaders—" Joos began.

"Are few and far between," Cornelia interrupted. "There are so few trained ministers to truly educate the people regarding the basic tenets of our faith. We all know the simple truth of justification by faith, but not many of us have a deep understanding of Scripture—

the kind of understanding that can enrich our fellowship with each other and with Christ."

Joos gaped at her. "What on earth are you talking about?"

"We need a clear confession of faith," Cornelia said, her voice growing animated. "Our people need a statement of beliefs to help them grasp their identity as reformed Christians. Don't you see? A clear sense of identity will strengthen the church."

Joos's brow furrowed. "And who would create such a confession?"

Cornelia drew in a deep breath. She had not planned to divulge her secret to her siblings just yet, but Joos had clambered onto the roof to fetch her without complaint and hadn't berated her once for her unladylike behaviour. "I would," she ventured.

"You!" he exclaimed.

Cornelia faced him, fury crimsoning her cheeks. "Why couldn't I?" she demanded.

Joos's eyes widened in disbelief. "You're a woman, and barely 17 to boot."

"And what if I am a woman?" Cornelia retorted. "Women have brains in their heads just as men do."

Joos's expression morphed from disbelief to shock to wonder. "You're serious," he breathed. He rubbed his forehead. "I have never heard of a woman drawing up a confession of faith before."

"Then you are clearly insufficiently educated," she said, smiling at him cheekily, "for several women have written confessions of faith—though admittedly, those have not been intended for adoption by an entire church."

"Joos! Cornelia! What are you doing up there? Joos, I told you to bring her down with you, not go up there and join her for a long conversation!" Susanna's voice floated up to them and Joos's face split into a grin.

"We better go back inside before she decides to come out here and get us," he said, inching towards the edge of the roof. He paused, turning back to eye Cornelia. "I certainly want to hear more about this outlandish idea of yours." His grin widened. "If any woman can accomplish such a feat, I am inclined to believe it will be my indomitable baby sister."

Spring, 1572

Cornelia chewed on the mangled end of her quill as she contemplated the sheet of paper before her. She had to get it just right—the words, the tone, the sentiment. It had to be coherent and fervent. Expelling an exasperated growl, she crumpled the paper before her and flung it across the room, where it fell among a growing pile of similarly discarded pages. Rising from her stool, she paced to the window, restless energy coursing through her.

She contemplated the clear skies outside her second-storey window, looking over the gabled rooftops to drink in the strip of azure ocean beyond. The day beckoned her to step into its warmth for a frolic. Cornelia sighed. She couldn't afford to frolic—not until she had perfected the precious document she had been working on for years. When she had first explained her idea to her siblings, Susanna and Joos thought she had lost her mind. For an anguished moment, Cornelia had wondered if they were right, but after prayerful consideration she felt compelled to write.

"We need this! The church needs this! And I am so close to completion," she had told her siblings a week ago when Susanna had complained that all she did was burrow in her bedroom to write.

"But should you be the one to provide it?" Susanna had demanded, eyeing her with a raised brow. "You, a 19-year-old girl? Do you really believe you can provide the reformed church in Zeeland with a confession of faith?"

Her sister's scepticism stung, but Cornelia understood her sentiments and her fear. Susanna did not want her to face the crushing disappointment of failure. In truth, it seemed impossible that a woman as young as she could produce something so momentous—and yet, why not? And if not her, then who?

Cornelia sank onto her stool once more, reaching for the small pamphlet that lay on her desk. She flipped it open, scanning the neat rows of print. It was the confession of the martyred reformist hero Guido de Brès—Walloon pastor, disciple of the great John Calvin and unhappy victim of the ruthless Spanish Inquisition. He was the man who had inspired Cornelia to produce her own confession of faith.

She was deeply engrossed, re-reading his harrowing but faithful testimony, when thudding footsteps on the stairs jolted her into the present. The door to her bedroom burst open, sending her pile of discarded papers fluttering as Joos barged into the room, Susanna on his heels.

"What is it?" she asked, leaping to her feet. De Brès's confession fell heedlessly to her desk.

"The Sea Beggars have taken Den Briel," Joos said, his voice hoarse with emotion.

Cornelia's eyes widened. "What?" she whispered.

Susanna let out a strangled sound that was half-laugh, half-sob. "It's true," she said, elbowing her way past Joos to stand before Cornelia, tears shimmering in her eyes. "They've taken Den Briel and evicted the Spanish!" Susanna threw her arms around Cornelia and burst into tears.

Cornelia's eyes remained fixed on her brother's face, disbelief warring with elation. He nodded his confirmation, then smiled. Cornelia threw her arms around her sister with a joyful whoop and whirled her around the room.

The Sea Beggars were reformist revolutionaries who had taken up arms to wrest the Dutch people from Spanish control. Taxes were oppressive and thousands had been burned or buried alive by order of the Spanish Inquisition, which wielded its power throughout the Low Countries. There had been more martyrs here than anywhere in Christendom—of this they were all certain. Capturing the strategic seaport of Den Briel was a tremendous victory for the resistance, signalling not only the hope of independence from Spain, but also the hope of religious liberty.

"This is just the beginning," Cornelia whispered to her sister, as they came to a halt in the centre of the room, sobbing and clinging to each other. "This is just the beginning. Soon we will be free to worship God without fear of death or punishment. Soon we will be able to organise our own churches and meet in public."

Susanna leaned back, wiping her damp cheeks. "You know what that means, don't you?" she asked tremulously.

Cornelia shook her head. "No, what?"

Susanna grinned. "It means the church will need a confession of faith stating its beliefs."

Cornelia's lips trembled as realisation swept over her. "You really think I can do it?" she whispered.

Joos strode over to them, enveloping them both in an embrace. "We really think you can," he whispered back, laying his cheek atop her head.

The night before she presented her confession to the leaders of the church, Cornelia couldn't sleep. She paced about her room restlessly, went downstairs to rummage in the kitchen for something to eat, woke up her siblings and generally wreaked havoc in their usually quiet home.

She understood the importance of what she was about to do, and a part of her trembled. What if they thought it was rubbish? Or worse still, what if they thought she was insolent? There were so few trained minsters in their province of Zeeland. Even fewer men, let alone women, who were equipped to write a confession of this sort. She was only 19 and a woman, but she knew that if the church leaders accepted it, the document could prove tremendously useful.

When dawn broke over the horizon, Cornelia instructed the servants to draw her a bath. Susanna came in to help dry her hair and arrange it. She put on her best dress, donned her bonnet and took up her confession. Then, like a Sea Beggar going to war, she followed her siblings to the small home that served as a church.

When she stood up to read her confession, the silence was so thick she feared it would suffocate her. The silence continued long after she finished reading. Finally, the head elder of the church rose, his brow hovering low over his pinched eyes.

"Did you write that yourself, Sister Teellinck?" he asked.

"I did, sir," she said quietly. "I wished to make known to this congregation and others like us not only what I believe but why my faith differs from that of Romanists. I believe that as a congregation we should band together in unity, now more than ever, when war surrounds us and Spain means to crush us, body and spirit." She looked at the small, stunned congregation, imploringly. "Now we must know what we believe. We must be able to give a reason for the hope that is within us without fear or shame."

"May I see the document?" the elder asked, holding out his hand.

Cornelia slipped past her sister, who hurriedly reached out to squeeze her fingers. She handed the folded sheaf of papers to the elder, twisting her hands nervously as he read it.

"You have signed your name here," he observed, raising his eyes in question.

Cornelia nodded. "I have," she acknowledged. "Not as a mark of pride, but rather as a mark of courage. I want everyone to know what I believe, even if that exposes me to ridicule or persecution. My Lord was not ashamed of me, and I do not want to be ashamed of Him."

The elder nodded, folded the sheaf, then held it out to her. "Have you made copies?"

Cornelia's eyes widened. "No, sir, I have not. I only just finished it and—"

"We will need copies," he said, nodding to someone behind her.

Cornelia turned to see that he was staring directly at her brother. Joos scrambled to his feet, nodding.

"I will see it done," he said.

"Good." The elder clapped his hands together with a smile. "You have done us all proud, Sister Teellinck," he said. "On this eve of change, you have given us a rallying cry, a confession that can unite us as one church as we face the long road to liberation."

Cornelia offered him a tremulous smile, swallowing past the tightness in her throat. "I pray that God will use my words to further His kingdom," she whispered.

The elder held her gaze steadily. "I believe He will, Sister," he said gravely. "I believe He will."

Cornelia Teellinck and her siblings were among the earliest converts to Protestantism in Zeeland, the southernmost province of what would later become the Dutch Republic. The Low Countries—an area that today spans the Netherlands and parts of Belgium—had been under Spanish rule for over a century.

In 1566, the Low Countries experienced what is now known as the "Wonder Year," when Protestant preaching spread rapidly throughout the country. There is evidence of an underground church in Zierikzee in 1568, and open-air preachers, known as hedge preachers, were active in nearby Middelburg. By 1570, the Teellinck siblings had converted to Protestantism and owned a Bible. They also had access to other Protestant devotional literature, which Cornelia relied on heavily to compose her own work. In 1572, when the Port of Den Briel was captured by Protestants, marking the first victory over the Spanish, Cornelia Teellinck, then aged only 19, presented a written confession of faith to the small church in Zierikzee. This document was circulated throughout the churches in Zeeland and was a significant step towards establishing the Dutch Reformed Church in this region.

Cornelia was married for two years to Antonie Limmens, and they had a daughter, Katrijnken. Cornelia died in 1576, at the age of 23, five weeks after her husband's death. Her daughter was raised by Susanna and Joos Teellinck. For 30 years following her death, Cornelia's work was circulated in manuscript form. Then, in 1607, Susanna penned a biographical introduction about her sister and prepared her work for publication. The book was published by three printers between 1607 and 1625, in at least five editions.

5

Marie Dentière

A TIME TO SPEAK

Geneva, Switzerland
Summer, 1535

"You know," Antoine Froment said to his wife as they were sorting newly arrived goods in the back of their small shop, "we would get into a lot less trouble if you tried to keep your mouth shut."

Marie paused in the act of prying a lid off a barrel to consider this. "If I did that, I wouldn't recognise myself," she said, before going back to work on the lid.

Antoine laughed, even as he shook his head.

"Besides," Marie continued with a grunt as she leaned against her crowbar, "I don't always use my mouth to speak. More often than not, I use my pen."

Antoine grinned as he hurried over to her to help her with the stubborn barrel lid. Once it was removed, they began scooping grain into smaller sacks, ready for sale.

"Speaking of keeping my mouth shut," Marie began after a prolonged silence, "I was thinking of accepting the offer of a speaking engagement."

Beside her, Antoine tensed, then straightened up from the barrel to peer at her. "Who invited you to speak?" he asked cautiously.

Marie shrugged, continuing to shovel grain fastidiously into her sack. "It was not so much an invitation as a suggestion," she ventured.

Antoine groaned. "It's in some controversial place, isn't it?" He tossed his small trowel back into the barrel as he turned to face her. "Where is it? A convent?" He stared at Marie, waiting for an answer, but she avoided his gaze. "Well?" he prompted.

Marie bit her lip and poured more grain into an already bulging sack. Finally, unable to bear the silence, Antoine took the scoop away from her, forcing her to turn to him. She feigned outrage and grabbed the scoop out of his hand.

"Yes," she admitted. "It is at a convent."

"Oh, for heaven's sake!" he muttered, running a hand through his hair as he began to pace. "We have had enough trouble in Geneva to last us several lifetimes. Will you now stir up more by going to preach to nuns?"

"I was a nun too, remember?" she snapped, tossing down her scoop in irritation. She faced him, planting her hands on her hips, a gesture that signalled her intractable resolve. Antoine sighed in defeat.

"Why would you want to place yourself in such a precarious position?" he asked, changing tactics in the hope of appealing to her reason. *If she has any left in that head of hers*, he thought wryly, appraising her.

"Because someone placed themselves in that position for me," she countered.

"Did someone really preach to you inside the Augustinian convent in Tournai?" Antoine asked dubiously.

Marie hesitated. "Not exactly," she admitted, "but someone made a dangerous choice to send us the truth. If I had not heard the gospel, I would never have known Christ. I would never have been free. I would still be shackled to a lifetime of anxious ritual. But look at me now, Antoine." Her wide-eyed gaze turned imploring. "I am free because someone was brave enough to share the gospel with a nun like me. How can I refuse to do the same when I may be the instrument Christ uses to liberate someone else?"

Antoine dropped his face into his hands, feeling as though he was the one who had lost his reason. Of course, she must preach to the nuns. How could she not? Yet, he understood the risks—not only of censure, ridicule and public humiliation, but also of bodily harm.

"If you go, you expose yourself to danger," he said, lifting his head from his hands. He knew he was stating the obvious, but he felt the need to make sure she was aware of the risks.

"If I go, I expose others to the beauty of Christ's salvation," Marie countered. "Do you not think that's worth a world of danger?"

Antoine pursed his lips before unleashing his final, most pressing argument. "Women do not preach in public, my love," he said softly.

Marie narrowed her eyes. "Then I shall be the first."

Geneva had been embroiled in a prolonged religious war—one that was as bloody as it was brutal. But of late it had been marked more by intellectual conflict than physical warfare. The reformist thinkers who had sought refuge within its walls had been determined to liberate it from the clutches of the Catholic Duke of Savoy. The struggle was protracted, unpleasant and often dangerous. The duke had been dispatched two years previously, and his removal had initiated the difficult task of convincing the rest of the citizenry to accept the Reformation.

Marie was in the thick of all this because Antoine was in the thick of it. He was a merchant by trade but a minister by calling, often ascending the pulpit to preach the gospel. The Catholics called him a heretic because he spoke from Scripture. The reformists called him greedy because he operated a profitable business. Antoine and Marie turned a deaf ear to the censure and focused on doing what God called them to do. Still, as Marie prepared to storm the gates of Poor Clare's Convent with their friend William Farel, Antoine couldn't help but worry.

"How on earth did Farel manage to wrangle an invitation?" Antoine muttered at breakfast on the morning in question. Marie bustled about the table, ensuring that her husband and five children ate their food without incident.

"With all the upheaval in the city, some are cautiously willing to hear what reformists have to say," Marie replied, as she leaned over to scrub her small son's face and mop up a patch of spilled milk on the rough table.

She cast a glance at Antoine, who sat watching her, his breakfast forgotten before him. He and William Farel were both French exiles who had fled to Switzerland to evade persecution in their homeland. Together with other reformers, they had worked tirelessly to bring the Reformation to Geneva. Now Farel's vision was to create a truly reformist city. Marie thought Strasbourg already resembled that description, but Farel had grander plans for Geneva.

Marie returned her attention to the small urchin before her, smiled down at him, then placed a kiss on his warm cheek. She cast a sideways glance at her husband, who had returned to chewing his porridge. He was a good man, a good provider, but above all a good partner in ministry who didn't seem to mind her outspoken ways. Much.

"Are you really opposed to my going to the convent?" she asked as she began to scrub the large porridge pot languishing in the washbasin.

"Not opposed," Antoine said slowly. "I simply want to make sure that you understand the risks involved."

"Everything we have done over the past several years has involved risk," Marie countered, turning to face him with her hands immersed in dirty dishwater. She raised her shoulder to brush away a stray strand of hair that clung to her face, watching her husband's reaction.

"That is true," he agreed. Then, looking at her appraisingly, he continued, "Have you prepared yourself for the possibility that the nuns may not like what you have to say?"

Marie stared at him in disbelief. "Why would they not wish to be set free?"

"Because freedom can be daunting to those who have grown accustomed to their bonds. You are going to upset their well-ordered lives by forcing them to confront truths they'd rather ignore." He rose, moving to stand before her. "I just want you to temper your expectations," he said gently. "They may not be willing to embrace the gospel as enthusiastically as you once did."

Marie stared at him, shaking her head. "Such thinking," she declared staunchly, "is incomprehensible."

Antoine simply sighed and returned to his porridge.

Marie breathed in the familiar scents of incense, candle wax and musty leather as she followed Monsieur Farel into the library of Poor Clare's Convent. He had thought she would be a good ambassador for the Reformation to the nuns in the cloister. After all, she had once been a nun herself. Marie wholeheartedly agreed with his assessment, despite Antoine's cautions.

The nuns were gathered in the library. Monsieur Farel spoke to them briefly about justification by faith, then he motioned Marie forward.

"This is Madame Froment," he said, by way of introduction. "She is the wife of one of our best preachers, Monsieur Antoine Froment. They have five children."

The nuns absorbed this with stoic faces.

"She was once a nun like you," Farel stated. At this, Marie saw several sets of eyes widen.

"And then," Farel continued grandly, "she abandoned her vows. Shortly, after leaving the convent, she married a priest. She is a woman of great virtue. A true example of all that a reformist woman should be."

Scandalised gasps followed his announcement, and a sense of unease washed over Marie. Oblivious to the stir he was causing, Farel continued his rousing introduction, waxing lyrical as he enumerated

Marie's virtues as a wife and mother. The more he spoke, the thicker the silence became.

When Marie finally approached the lectern, the nuns looked like angry birds ready to gouge her eyes out. She was tempted to ask Farel to excuse her, but then she remembered who she was—Marie Dentière never cowered. Steeling her resolve, she opened the small Bible before her and began to preach the gospel.

That was the first scandalous thing she did that day—for a woman never preached in public. Unfortunately for Marie, it was not the *most* scandalous thing she did. What truly turned the tide against her was when she turned to Scripture to preach about the place, purpose and practicality of marriage. She urged the nuns to leave the convent's walls behind, in exchange for freedom in Christ and families in the world beyond.

When her sermon ended, she felt rather gratified. Her arguments had been powerful, scriptural, indestructible. She had urged truth upon the nuns—truth that had set her free and given her a joyful life, full of purpose. That was what she wanted for them all. Her mind had been so completely preoccupied with her sermon that she had not realised the animosity that had come to boiling point within the room.

Now, Marie stared wide-eyed at the nuns before her. If they had looked ready to gouge out her eyes when she had begun her sermon, they looked ready to feed her to the flames now.

"Jezebel!" one nun hissed.

"She is a woman of ill repute," another announced, "sent by the devil himself to entice us away from our true calling."

"What!" Marie exclaimed, unable to stop herself. "I have spoken to you from Scripture. How can you—"

"We have heard enough," said the abbess, standing.

"No! Wait!" Marie cried, raising her hand. "I am here because I have experienced the beauty of fellowship with Christ. It is a treasure I value more than life itself. How then can I bury that treasure when so many others—yourselves included—could be benefitted by it?" Marie's gaze turned imploring, even as the eyes of the nuns hardened in growing fury. "I am here to preach Christ. His love constrains me to speak. Don't you see? I cannot remain silent."

"Silence would have befitted you more than your rash and ill-advised speech, *Madame* Froment," the abbess spat out icily. "We do not need to hear Christ preached from the likes of you!"

Marie felt the blood drain from her face.

The abbess turned to Farel. "I think, Monsieur, that you have both overstayed your welcome. It is time to leave."

The setback at Poor Clare's Convent temporarily stunned Marie but did nothing to dissuade her.

"If they will not let me speak, then I will write," she told Antoine one morning, bustling about their shop gathering parchment, ink and quills. He watched her with a mixture of concern, affection and amusement.

"Have you retired from preaching, then?" he asked, his lips twitching.

Marie shot him a withering glare. "I will speak when the occasion arises, but I cannot sit around waiting for permission to preach the gospel. Christ has already bid me go and make disciples. I cannot be silent."

"Or still," Antoine drawled with a grin.

"You will have to care for the shop alone this morning," Marie called over her shoulder, hurrying up the narrow stairs that led to their living quarters.

Antoine watched her go. He had always known his wife was irrepressible. The truth burned within her, straining for expression. It would bring her as much grief as it did satisfaction, for he knew her determination would garner considerable opposition. Yet, it would also enrich countless lives. Shaking his head, he turned to open the shop for business.

Marie Dentière was born in Tournai (in modern Belgium) in 1495. She entered the Augustinian convent in Tournai at a young age but left in the early 1520s when Martin Luther's message of salvation by faith infiltrated the convent's walls. Marie made her way to Strasbourg, where she likely spent time with Matthew and Katharina Zell. There, she married Simon Robert, a Catholic priest turned Lutheran minister, and they had five children. Around this time, she began corresponding with Margaret of Navarre. One of Marie's later letters to Margaret was published, drawing criticism and praise in equal measure. In 1528, Marie and Simon Robert became the first Protestant couple commissioned to plant a church. After Simon's death in 1533, Marie and the children moved to Geneva, where she reconnected with Antoine Froment, a longstanding friend. They were married in 1535. Marie preached to the nuns at Poor Clare's Convent in August that year, drawing the ire of their abbess, Jeanne de Jussie, who later wrote a scathing denunciation against her. In 1536, she wrote The War and Deliverance of the City of Geneva, *a detailed account of the struggle between the reformers and the Catholic Duke of Savoy. Marie's writing was often confrontational, a style embraced by other prominent reformers in Geneva. She blazed a trail as a female preacher, writer and theologian, and she was respected by many contemporary reformers, including John Calvin. In 2002, she became the first and only woman featured on the Reformation Wall in Geneva, Switzerland.*

6

Jenny Geddes

RADICAL DISSENT

Edinburgh, Scotland
Summer, 1637

No self-respecting Scot could ever accept the rule of an English king.

"They can't be trusted," Jenny Geddes told her friend Mary one morning as they prepared Jenny's market stall for business.

Mary grunted as she hefted a crate of apples from the wagon tethered behind the flimsy wooden structure. "That is for sure and certain," she agreed, setting the crate down with a thud before straightening and stretching her back. "I'm getting too old for this," she muttered.

"Aren't we all?" Jenny agreed, unpacking the apples onto the straw-lined table that fronted the stall.

"But you can't escape the truth that this king of ours isn't English," Mary pointed out, reaching for the egg crate on the wagon. "He's Scots through and through."

Jenny waved a dismissive hand. "He may come from good Scottish stock," she conceded, "but look at him now, comfortably nestled in England without a care for any of his Scots subjects. You'd think he'd never ventured farther than the Humber the way he goes on."

Around them, other stallholders prepared for the day, bustling about with their wares. The familiar smells of peat and refuse stung their noses in the early morning air, which still retained a bite of iciness. Talking about the king was commonplace these days, especially since he had married a Romanist princess and begun to show signs of leaning away from the reformed faith.

"I don't mind if he slides back into the arms of the pope himself, as long as he leaves us to worship in peace," Mary said with a pained grunt as she hefted yet another crate.

"That's just it, isn't it?" Jenny countered. "He wants to control us all. Bring us to heel as though we were his personal hounds. I won't have it, I tell you." She pounded a fist on the table, now groaning beneath the weight of her wares, sending an apple flying.

Mary scrambled after the errant apple, while Jenny continued to unload the wagon. She then set out a pail of water for her mule and seated herself on the three-legged stool beside her stall.

"You're going to go to your grave with that stool," Mary grumbled motioning to it.

Jenny grinned as she shifted. "It's not my fault you don't want your own stool," she said. "Unlike you, I never have to worry about my back aching after a long day at the market."

Mary rolled her eyes before turning away. Jenny Geddes never went anywhere without her stool. She even carried it into St Giles' Kirk on a Sunday to hear the sermon. It was like a small pet, following her wherever she went.

The sun rose steadily over the city, awakening it until the streets were thronged with all manner of people. Jamie Shedden sauntered over to Jenny's stall about noon, his relaxed gait belying the excitement in his eyes.

"Well?" Jenny asked, eyeing him suspiciously as he came to a halt before her.

He reached for an apple, and she shot up to slap his hand away. "Be off with you!" she snapped.

He shrugged nonchalantly, eyeing her, then the apple. "I thought you might be feeling generous this morning," he said.

"And why would I?" Jenny asked.

He smiled slyly. "Because I have some news that might interest you."

She paused, pursing her lips and narrowing her eyes. "What kind of news?"

That was all the prompting Jamie Shedden needed. He leaned in, beckoning her forward. Mary scrambled over to them from her place behind the stall table.

"I've heard tell that changes are afoot," Jamie whispered ominously.

Jenny continued to regard him with steely eyed suspicion. "What kind of changes?' she challenged.

Jamie leaned even closer, dropping his voice to a whisper, though they were surrounded by so much noise it would have been impossible for anyone to overhear him. "There are rumours that the king and his archbishop, old Laud, have gotten together a new prayer book."

"And what does this new prayer book say?"

"They say that Laud has made it as Romanist as he can. Apparently, he means to take us all the way back to the papacy."

Jenny frowned. This was too much.

"Oh, pish!" Mary exclaimed. "To a Scot, anything the English Church does is as like the Roman Church as the papacy itself."

Jamie laughed. "Sure enough," he conceded. "But I'm telling you, this is different. They mean to make us Romanists again. Forcing us to have bishops and the like is one thing, but now they even want to change our prayers. I've heard tell that listening to the new Book of Common Prayer is no different than listening to a mass."

"God preserve us!" Mary breathed.

Jenny rubbed her chin, then turned to pace before the stall. The Scots Kirk was free—it always had been. And now, here was the king trying to bind it to his whims.

"We can't allow it," she finally said, whirling to face them. "We can't allow the king to come in here with his fancy false religion and try to turn us away from the foundation of our faith. We owe our allegiance to none but God. If the king thinks he can change that, he had better think again!"

Mary and Jamie blinked at her, frozen in shock.

"Well?" Jenny said, waving a hand in the air. "Are we really going to just roll over and let them ride over us?"

Jamie scratched behind his ear, shifting uncomfortably. "But what are we going to do?" he asked. "We're poor folk struggling to put food on our tables. We're no match for the king."

Jenny leaned around him to grab an apple from the dwindling pile. "No, lad," she corrected, tossing the fruit to him with a grim smile. "It's the king who's no match for us."

St Giles' Cathedral, Edinburgh, Scotland
July 23, 1637

Jenny marched into the Sunday service like a mercenary going to war, her stool tucked beneath her arm. Mary trailed behind her, darting nervous glances at Jenny's back. "You aren't going to do anything foolish, are you?" she asked.

Jenny glanced at her over her shoulder. "Have you ever known me to do anything foolish?" she demanded.

Mary simply rolled her eyes. They wove through the crowd to their usual spot, where Jenny set her stool down on the straw-lined floor and lowered herself onto it with a grunt. Mary lowered herself to the floor beside Jenny, tucking her feet beneath the tattered hem of her gown.

"You need to get yourself a stool," Jenny said, eyeing Mary as she awkwardly tried to situate herself amid the prickly straw.

"I can't be troubled carrying it around as though it were a third arm," Mary grumbled. She leaned back against a stone pillar, breathing out a relieved sigh. "Goodness but it's been a long week," she muttered, closing her eyes as she reached around to rub her lower back.

Jenny turned to face the imposing stained-glass windows before her, taking in the comforting familiarity of the grand old kirk. She couldn't imagine it being filled with images or beclouded with incense as it had once been so long ago. It wouldn't come to that again if she had anything to say about it.

The Dean of Edinburgh, James Hannay, stepped forward to begin the service, opening the Book of Common Prayer to read. As his droning voice filled the cathedral, Jenny's eyes flew open. With each line he read, she felt fire course through her limbs. She could scarcely believe their audacity—but they had done it. The king and old Bishop Laud had rearranged the Book of Common Prayer, turning it into a recitation of the mass.

Jenny shot to her feet, hefted her stool over her head and flung it directly at the unsuspecting dean's head.

"The devil give you colic!" she shouted. "Dare you recite the mass in my ear? You false thief!"

The dean emitted a strangled cry before ducking away from the three-legged projectile hurtling towards him. The stool flew over his head, clattering to the floor behind him. Mary squealed and the congregation erupted in a chorus of gasps.

The dean rose from his crouch, his face flushed with indignation. He opened his mouth to speak, but before he could do so, he was struck squarely in the face with a book. Gasping, he staggered back, one hand raised to shield himself, but it did him no good for he was immediately struck in the chest with a rotten apple. He watched as the putrid mass slid down his robes, then he gaped at the congregation.

Before he could utter a word, chaos erupted like the roar of a canon's blast. The congregation rose as one body, hurling stools, books, fruit—anything they could get their hands on—while shouting denunciations against the dean, the king, the Archbishop of Canterbury and, most notably, the heretical new prayer book.

Mary turned to Jenny who stood frozen in shock, staring at the commotion about her. "Good heavens, Jenny!" she shouted above the tumult. "You've gone and started a riot!"

Edinburgh, Scotland
February, 1638

A muted tap sent Jenny flying to answer her door. She cracked it open, peering out to find Jamie on the other side. Jenny beckoned him inside.

"Were you followed?" she asked, shutting the door behind him.

"If anyone wanted to harm you, they'd have done so by now," he commented dryly. "Besides, I don't think the dean knows who threw that stool and started the riot."

Jenny sank onto a chair before her low-burning hearth, tugging her shawl tightly around her shoulders. "I wasn't trying to start a riot," she muttered defensively.

Jamie sank to the floor before her, drawing up his knees as he held his hands to the flames.

"I doubt you were trying to be peaceful," he countered. "At the very least, you were hoping to do the Dean of Edinburgh serious bodily harm." He shot her a sideways glance and she offered him a small smile.

"I wasn't trying to kill him," she said.

He shook his head. "No, but you were trying to clip him hard enough to knock some sense into him."

"Yes, I won't deny that."

Jamie's face was serious as he turned to face her. "Well, your fit of righteous indignation might not have been the wisest course of action or the most decorous, but it has led to some much-needed change."

Jenny leaned forward, her eyes wide. "They've done it, then?" she breathed.

He nodded, a slow grin spreading across his face. "That they have. I've just come from Greyfriars."

Jenny's eyes closed as she lifted her hands in prayer. "Thanks be to God," she murmured.

"We'll have to see if the king honours the agreement," Jamie cautioned. "You know what he's like—as slippery as an eel and craftier than a fox. But for now, he's signed the National Covenant, promising to allow the Scots Kirk freedom."

Jenny laughed joyfully. "Oh, Jamie, what a victory! Thanks be to God that the Scottish lords were brave enough to stand up to the king and demand religious freedom."

"Yes," Jamie agreed solemnly, though his eyes glinted with humour. "And just think, it all started with a feisty woman throwing her stool in church."

Jenny grinned at him. "There's something to be said for taking action."

He rolled his eyes, then went back to warming his hands by the hearth. "Just make sure that next time you're displeased with me, you use your words, not your furniture."

Not much is known about Jenny Geddes apart from her dramatic confrontation with the Dean of Edinburgh inside St Giles' Cathedral in July, 1637. She was likely born around the year 1600 and worked as a stallholder at the Edinburgh market. She was poor, attended services regularly and took her stool with her to church. The words she spoke when she hurled her stool at the dean are recorded in history. A replica of her stool is on display inside St Giles' Cathedral today, along with a description of her unconventional protest. Her actions led to seven months of rioting in Edinburgh, precipitating the signing of the National Covenant in 1638, a document that ensured the freedom of the Scottish Church and halted the compromising reforms that Charles I, King of England and Scotland, was attempting to make.

7

Elizabeth Cruciger

A SONG OF SOLACE

Premonstratensian Convent, Belbuck Abbey,
Treptow, Pomerania
Winter, 1521

The sound of singing beckoned to Elizabeth. She followed it to the chapel where lauds—the canonical hour of prayer at daybreak—was beginning. Inside, she breathed in the familiar fragrance of incense, candle wax and old wood, her senses swimming as the heady melody of chanted prayer washed over her. The music soothed her, enveloping her in its steady cadence.

Elizabeth never missed these hours. The music ebbed and flowed within her like a living thing, filling her with peace as nothing else could. There were many things she disliked about being a nun, many times she wondered what life might be like outside the damp stone walls of the abbey, but every time she imagined herself away from this place, one thought drew her back—how could she breathe without music?

When lauds ended, Elizabeth followed the other nuns out of the chapel. Despondency returned to stalk her like an animal. The music always granted her a reprieve from reality. It allowed her to escape the despair that rushed at her when she remembered the cage she lived in—not only the abbey, but the entirety of Christendom.

A line from the Psalms came to her—*Whither shall I flee from Thy presence?* It caused a shiver to course through her. She could never escape God's wrath. She could never flee from His terrifying presence, nor His repeated reminders of her depravity. She could never appease Him, no matter how hard she tried. Only music granted her relief. It made her forget, if only for a moment, that she had been weighed in God's balances and found wanting.

Music was her refuge. Beyond its borders, she occupied a barren landscape.

Later that day, Elizabeth was waylaid by Veronika Baumgartner, who dragged her into an alcove and pressed her against the cold stone.

"What on earth?" Elizabeth gasped, her hand fluttering to her chest as she tried to regain her composure. "Veronika! You nearly sent me to my grave! What are you doing?"

"*Shhh!*" Veronika whispered, her big eyes darting everywhere at once.

Trepidation bubbled inside Elizabeth. Since the rebel monk Luther had begun to disseminate his ideas throughout Christendom, the abbey had been shrouded with tension. Both the monks in the monastery and the nuns in the convent had been warned against opening their ears to his teachings.

"Will you come to a meeting?" Veronika whispered.

"Is this about Luther?" Elizabeth asked, planting her hands on her hips and getting straight to the point. "Because if it is—"

"It is," Veronika confirmed, cutting her off. "But you must come. One of the monks from next door has sent us a bundle of notes from his lectures with Herr Bugenhagen."

Herr Bugenhagen was a priest who frequently lectured at the monastery next door. He had always been staunchly in favour of the church. But recently, rumours had begun to circulate among the nuns that he was teaching the monks Luther's doctrines.

"What?" Elizabeth squeaked, scandalised. "How did he even get it across?"

"It doesn't matter how they smuggled it here—only that they did," Veronika replied, her fingers digging into Elizabeth's arm. "Will you come?"

Elizabeth chewed her lip as she contemplated the best course of action. If they were caught, they could all land in a heap of trouble. On the other hand, if they managed to keep their meetings secret, she could satisfy her curiosity about what the German monk had to say and be done with it.

She drew in a deep breath as she contemplated yet another facet of this situation. Luther was a heretic. The wrath of God fell heavily upon heretics. Elizabeth had spent her life trying to evade the wrath of God, which meant that associating with a heretic was not only foolish but dangerous.

"Well?" Veronika demanded as the silence stretched interminably.

Elizabeth squeezed her eyes shut, rubbed her forehead, and then in a reckless rush decided to risk it.

"What time and where?" she asked, rolling her eyes at Veronika's muffled squeal of delight.

The small group that met to discuss the heretical musings of John Bugenhagen parted ways conflicted. Over the following weeks, Elizabeth stumbled through the familiar ritual of convent life in a daze. Her inability to concentrate, especially during the canonical hours of prayer caused concern. Several older nuns stopped to ask if she was well. She wanted to tell them that she was not well, that she feared nothing in her life would ever be well again.

Herr Bugenhagen had shared strange ideas about salvation, about Christ, about Scripture. Elizabeth felt like a skein of wool slowly unspooling. She could not sleep, could not eat, could not sing. She spent hours in the library poring over the Bible chained there, reading feverishly until the candles burned low and the librarian came to chase her away.

Then the chaos began to clarify into understanding, then into peace, as she saw Jesus—the power of His love, the beauty of His sacrifice. The image of Christ dying for a sinner like her gradually washed away her fear of an angry God. God was not angry, she realised. God was merciful. And still more wondrous, God was the very essence of love.

Suddenly, music became a vehicle of expression rather than a portal of escape. She no longer leaned on it like a lame woman leaning on her crutch. Instead, she used it as a gift to glorify the Giver. She began to write her thoughts on scraps of parchment, not in prose but in verse, because her brain functioned in rhythm, meter, cadence and melody. She wrote poem after poem, using this form of expression to make sense of what was being revealed to her in Scripture.

One night, nibbling on the end of her quill, she contemplated what she had read that day as she compared Herr Bugenhagen's notes to the scriptural references he had quoted. Then she wrote:

> He is the Star of Morning,
> whose beams afar are soaring,
> above all other lights.
> Now at the end of ages,
> He comes, a human born,
> we poor received God's wages:
> Sin's judgment from us torn.

She paused here, as tears welled in her eyes. She could hardly believe it. She had laboured beneath a cloud of despair for so long, and now her hopelessness had been cut away by the light of Christ's love as easily as a hot knife slicing through butter.

She dipped her quill in the well of ink once more, contemplating her next words, when a knock sounded on her door. Her head snapped up, eyes wide, as she took in the notes strewn across her desk.

"Who is it?" she called, dropping her quill, as she hastily gathered the loose paper into a bundle.

"Els, it's me."

Relief flooded through Elizabeth at the sound of Veronika's voice. Dropping her bundle of papers, she walked to the door and cracked it open.

"No-one else is in sight," Veronika assured her, slipping into the room. She laughed when she took in the pile of papers, the discarded quill and the ink bottle knocked askew. "Were you writing again?"

"Yes," Elizabeth answered, absently rubbing at a stubborn ink stain on her finger. "And I was terrified that it was the abbess interrupting my clandestine foray into reformist poetry."

"Your secret is safe with me," Veronika assured her with a grin. But her smile quickly turned into a frown.

"What is it?" Elizabeth asked.

"Herr Bugenhagen has left," she said quietly.

Elizabeth's eyes widened in surprise. "Left?" she repeated. "Where has he gone?"

Veronika sank onto Elizabeth's cot with a shrug, while Elizabeth perched on the stool she had recently vacated. "No-one knows. He didn't leave alone though; several other monks have gone with him. Some say he has gone to Wittenberg to find Luther."

"What!" Elizabeth exclaimed. "Gone to find Luther? But what about us?"

They all depended on Herr Bugenhagen's lectures. If he was not preaching to the monks, and if the monks didn't smuggle his notes to the nuns, then how could any of them learn more?

"What are we to do?" Elizabeth wondered.

Veronika's mouth tipped up in a wry smile. "Perhaps we should set off to find Luther as well."

Wittenberg, Germany
Spring, 1524

"Are you a writer?"

The words, quietly spoken in her ear by a deep voice, caused Elizabeth to jump. She turned to face the young man beside her, raising an inquiring eyebrow not only at his question but also his impertinence in addressing her so familiarly in public. The man seemed unfazed by her ire, raising a questioning eyebrow of his own as he nodded towards her hands. Elizabeth glanced down and immediately noticed the tell-tale smudge of ink on her forefinger.

"I am." She paused, frowning. "I write poetry."

Elizabeth kept her eyes fixed on the bowl before her on the enormous table in the dining hall of the Black Cloister. It had once been an Augustinian monastery, but now it housed Herr Luther and numerous scholars, refugees and students from various parts of Germany.

"Poetry," the young man beside her repeated. He pretended to ponder this, before flashing her a small smile. "Are you any good?"

She glared at him, mustering her haughtiest expression. "It is not wise to praise oneself."

"False humility is not a mark of virtue," he responded with a smirk.

"You are impertinent, sir!" Elizabeth hissed.

"And you, fräulein, have not told me your name," he responded smoothly.

Appalled, Elizabeth turned back to her bowl, picked up her spoon and began ladling broth into her mouth with a vengeance. The nerve of the man! Who did he think he was? Disturbing her peace and behaving in such an improper manner.

"My name is Caspar," he said, picking up his own spoon and lazily stirring his broth.

Elizabeth darted a glance at him from the corner of her eye, huffed out a small breath and continued eating.

"Do you often join Dr Luther's table talk?" he continued pleasantly.

Elizabeth gritted her teeth. This was all highly inappropriate. If she were still in the convent—

She paused here, spoon suspended in the air before her mouth. She was no longer in the convent. She had left two years ago, following Herr Bugenhagen here to Wittenberg, where she now lived with him and his wife Walpurga. She had immersed herself in Scripture, completely embraced the gospel and inserted herself into the reformist circle in Wittenberg. She was free of her former vows. It was perfectly acceptable to converse with this young man—in fact it was probably wise to do so, unless she wished to remain unmarried.

Forcing herself to draw in a deep breath, Elizabeth lowered her spoon, turned to face the man and offered him a strained smile. "I'm Elizabeth von Meseritz, formerly a nun from Pomerania."

Caspar grinned, laid down his spoon and rested his forearms on the table before him. "I'm Caspar Cruciger, hopeful theologian and current student of Dr Luther's at the university."

Elizabeth nodded primly. "I am pleased to meet you, Herr Cruciger."

Caspar's grin widened. "And I am charmed to meet you, Fräulein von Meseritz. So tell me, what was it like to live in a cloister?"

Summer, 1524

When Elizabeth considered her life, she was both awed by the goodness of God and warmed by His love. She had finally finished her first hymn—as much a theological exploration as it was a song of praise to her beloved, Jesus Christ.

She had written it at Dr Luther's urging, for he believed that hymns could spread the gospel as effectively as sermons. She had submitted it to Dr Luther some weeks ago to be added to a collection of hymns, written by him and other men, that he was compiling for a hymnal. Now she awaited news of what would become of her music.

A knock on her chamber door was followed by Caspar's steady voice. "Els, are you ready?"

Elizabeth glanced up to see him framed in her doorway, dressed for the day before them. She offered him a smile, rose from her desk and extended her hand to clasp his proffered arm.

"I'm ready," she said.

Together, they walked into the small parlour of Herr Bugenhagen's home, where Dr Luther stood by the fireplace, ready to officiate their wedding ceremony. It was a quick and solemn affair. Dr Luther read to Caspar from Genesis 3:19, gravely admonishing him, "In the sweat of thy face though shalt eat bread." Then turning to Elizabeth, he intoned with equal gravity, "In sorrow thou shalt bring forth children." He then put rings on their fingers, offered a prayer and solemnised their union with the startling words, "Be fruitful and multiply!" Elizabeth blushed hotly, while Caspar coughed, pressed his fist to his mouth and tried unsuccessfully to quell his laughter.

At the small wedding luncheon, which was sparsely attended but lavishly catered thanks to generous amounts of food procured by Herr Bugenhagen and his wife, Caspar slipped a small, wrapped parcel towards Elizabeth.

Her face widened into a delighted smile. "What's this?" she asked, snatching it up and pulling away the string that bound the rough cloth.

"A small wedding gift," he said, watching her intently as she peeled away the cloth to reveal a small book beneath. Elizabeth's eyes widened as her fingers brushed over the words inscribed on the cover.

"*Erfurt Enchiridion*," she read softly.

"It is the hymnal Dr Luther was compiling," Caspar said, his eyes still fixed on her face.

She nodded, then realisation dawned.

Caspar smiled, nodding back at her. "Open it," he encouraged.

With trembling fingers she opened the book, turning the pages until she came to the hymn she sought—the one she had written, the one that reflected the depth of her love and devotion to Christ. The summary of her understanding of the gospel.

"The only woman to be included in the hymnal," he said, his voice full of pride.

Elizabeth laughed.

"Elizabeth Cruciger," Caspar continued, "female hymn writer of the new reformist movement." He paused. "How does that sound?"

"I like it," she said, grinning at him. "I like it very much."

Elizabeth Cruciger (neé von Meseritz) was born around the year 1500 to a wealthy noble family on the estate of Meseritz in Pomerania (part of modern-day Poland). She entered a convent as a child and heard about the gospel from John Bugenhagen, a young preacher appointed to preach to the monks at the Premonstratensian monastery within the Belbuck Abbey complex. After leaving the convent, she lived with Bugenhagen and his wife Walpurga before her marriage to Caspar Cruciger, who eventually became a member of the theological faculty at the University of Wittenberg. The Erfurt Enchiridion *was published in 1524, the year of their marriage. It was the second Lutheran hymnal and contained about 25 hymns. Elizabeth has the honour of being the Reformation's first female hymn writer. She was the only woman whose work was featured in the hymnal. She died in 1535.*

8

Anna Bullinger

LOVE THAT SUFFERS LONG

Ottenbach Convent, Zurich, Switzerland
Summer, 1522

Anna Adlischweiler felt besieged, with no means to defend or extricate herself. In a corner of the room, her mother was praying as feverishly as if casting Beelzebub himself out of their midst. Her hands moved with practised precision over the wooden cross she was clutching. Anna watched her mother with a mixture of resignation and dread. Frau Adlischweiler was a pious woman, known for her fervent devotion to the church—a devotion that often made her overbearing. Anna already feared the wrath of God; the added burden of fearing her mother's wrath repeatedly threatened to undo her.

Expelling a sigh, Anna moved to her mother's side and laid a gentle hand on her shoulder. "We must go, Mother," she said softly, urging the frail woman to her feet.

Her mother was a nervous woman, who had been ill for much of Anna's life. When Anna's father passed away a decade ago, her mother had given Anna to the convent. Soon after, she had entered its confines herself—as an invalid, not a nun—depending on the sisters, and later on her daughter, for care.

Anna had only the rigid routines of cloistered life to provide relief from her mother's constant demands. They were her oasis—and now they were under threat. Anna's fingers clenched convulsively on her mother's arm as she thought of the heretic who had entered her sanctuary. The man who had set her mother to praying so desperately. Her bruising grip caused her mother to yelp in surprise, and Anna apologised profusely, loosening her grip on her mother's fragile bones.

"No sense bruising me because you are angry with that man," her mother grumbled, rubbing her arm sullenly.

"I am sorry," Anna repeated, gentling her grip further.

"We don't have to attend his preaching, you know," her mother added as they approached the doors of the chapel.

"I know," Anna mumbled, but any overt dissent would be noted by the city councilmen who had sent this preacher to them. Considering the upheaval this man's presence threatened to cause them, Anna didn't want to court any more trouble. Caring for her mother absorbed what little strength she had; she couldn't spare a drop of it to set herself against the plans of powerful men.

They found the entire convent seated inside the chapel, glowering at the man who stood before the altar holding a small book in his hand. When her mother caught sight of him, she bristled.

"May God send you straight to the pits of hell, Herr Zwingli!" she shouted, her thin voice crackling.

Anna gaped at her in mortification, hustling her into a pew and pushing her down to sit with more force than necessary. Her mother grunted, then leaned into the aisle to throw another barb at the startled Zwingli.

"We don't want your heresy here!" she yelled, waving a fist in the air.

"Mother!" Anna admonished, dragging her back into the pew and clutching her arm to keep her still.

"What?" her mother demanded, loud enough for the whole chapel to hear. "He wants to know how we feel about him and I'm not afraid to speak the truth."

A murmur passed through the crowd, and Anna felt her face flush with enough heat to warm everyone in the building.

Having overcome his initial shock, Zwingli smiled at Anna's mother, then raised his Bible into the air, shouting, "If God sends me to the pits of hell for preaching from Scripture, then He will have to send St Peter and St Paul along with me."

More scandalised gasps echoed through the room.

"My sisters," he continued, glancing at Anna and her mother before looking around the congregation. "I have come to set you free from the bonds of darkness by revealing to you the marvellous light of the gospel."

A hostile silence, as thick as the incense that scented the air, descended over the sanctuary at his words. Anna knew he must be able to sense its oppressive weight, but instead of being daunted, he cheerfully opened his Bible and began to read from St Paul's epistle to the Romans.

Halfway through the sermon, Anna's mother slumped against her, snoring. But Anna hardly noticed her weight. She clung to every word that came from Zwingli's mouth, her fingers twitching with the desire to note down each salient point.

When the sermon ended, Anna sat there in stunned silence. The murmurs of the other nuns rose around her and her mother's snores rumbled in her ears, yet all these sounds were distant, like a nimbus hovering over the chapel. All Anna was aware of was the stupendous shift taking place in the vicinity of her heart.

Autumn, 1522

Zwingli's sermons replaced the tranquil regularity of convent life with enough turmoil to rival a papal crusade. The nuns pecked at each other like crows. Some, like Anna's mother, insisted that Zwingli was a devil in monk's clothing, while others, like Anna, studied his sermons with intense interest. Everyone had an opinion, and the breakdown of the convent seemed imminent.

Zwingli was granted permission by the city councillors to preach to them regularly, and Anna attended every sermon, taking notes and searching Scripture until, finally, much to her mother's dismay, she declared herself in favour of the Reformation.

"Who will pray for my soul when I am gone?" her mother screeched, when Anna admitted her convictions.

"I will pray for you while you are alive," Anna replied gently. "I will pray that you will accept the power and the grace of Christ and find salvation in Him."

"Salvation is found in the church alone," her mother retorted, smoothing agitated fingers over her crucifix. "I cannot bear it," she moaned, covering her face with her hand. "How can I bear the thought of my only child becoming a heretic?"

"I am not a heretic, Mama," Anna said, coming to crouch before her mother. She gently removed her hand from her face. "I am free."

Her mother shook her head. "You are not free," she insisted. "You are caught in the snare of the devil himself."

"I am free in Christ," Anna countered. "Free from the drudgery of my own works, free from the pretended authority of popes and priests. I am free to serve and worship God through Christ. He will save me. And He will save you, if you will allow Him."

Her mother burst into tears, then collapsed in a fit of nervous hysteria, screeching that Anna would burn in the pits of hell right alongside Zwingli. She was inconsolable for days, refusing to speak to Anna, refusing to eat.

Anna vacillated between guilt and anger, finally settling into a state of pained resignation. Their stand-off continued until Frau Adlischweiler was forced by her weakening health to accept her daughter's assistance. She grudgingly accepted Anna's convictions, though her hostility was unabated over the long months and years that followed.

Summer, 1527

After a particularly trying morning, Anna tucked her exhausted mother into bed before hurrying to the chapel for her meeting with Leo Juda. Soon after Zwingli's preaching, Herr Juda, one of Zwingli's disciples, had been appointed chaplain of the convent by the city council. He had faithfully ministered to the nuns, some of whom had bitterly opposed him, while others eagerly drank in his every word. Anna had been part of the latter group, grateful for his shepherding and counsel.

Over the years, Herr Juda's flock of nuns had slowly dwindled. Some abandoned the convent in search of a more orthodox sanctuary; others found husbands and left to build their own homes. Five years after Herr Zwingli first preached at the convent, Anna was the only remaining nun within its walls. She had been compelled to remain because of her mother's delicate health and because they had nowhere else to go. They had no magnanimous male relative or benefactor willing to care for them.

Anna often wondered why Herr Juda didn't abandon his duties at the convent—why he kept returning to minister to one lonely sheep. But perhaps that was why he kept returning. Because she was alone in her faith in this desolate place. Whatever the reason, she was grateful for his care.

When she entered the chapel, she saw that Herr Juda wasn't alone.

"Ah! Fräulein Adlischweiler," he greeted her.

"I am sorry I am late," she began. "My mother was feeling unwell." She paused before the two men, smiling shyly at the newcomer who stared back at her as though he had never seen a woman in his life.

Herr Juda glanced between them, cleared his throat, then elbowed his companion in the ribs. The man jumped.

"This is Henry Bullinger, my assistant," Herr Juda said. "I have brought him along to gain some pastoral experience." He glowered at Herr Bullinger, who had gone back to staring at Anna.

Anna smiled. "A pleasure to make your acquaintance, Herr Bullinger."

Henry cleared his throat and nodded. "A pleasure to meet you, fräulein." He coughed, shifted nervously on his feet, then grinned like a fool.

Anna giggled. Herr Juda groaned. And everything spiralled in a completely unexpected direction from there.

Four weeks after their first meeting, Henry Bullinger flouted convention by proposing to Anna himself. Propriety dictated that he enlist the help of a third party, but Henry didn't care to wait. Anna read his impassioned letter, which enunciated his feelings and urged his eligibility as a husband. But even as her heart leapt in elation, it sank to her toes in dread. Should Anna accept Henry's proposal—and she could not bring herself to refuse—it would surely fracture her already tenuous relationship with her mother.

"I love him," she said, tears streaming down her face as she watched her mother reading Henry's letter. "He is a good man and I see no reason why I cannot marry him."

She could have simply accepted his proposal without telling her mother, run away with him if she had wanted to, but Anna couldn't bring herself to abandon her mother—not when she grew weaker and more frail each day.

"You may as well kill me now," Frau Adlischweiler said with conviction, "for I would rather dig my own grave than allow you to marry a heretic. Do you hear me, Anna?" She rose to her feet, swaying, and clutched her crucifix in her fingers. "I would rather place myself beneath the ground than see my daughter marry one of those—reformers." She spat the word out as though it were poison.

Anna covered her mouth, pressing back a sob. She took a deep breath to calm herself as her mother tottered towards the open window on the far side of the room.

"I am one of those reformers, Mama," she said finally, when she had command of her voice.

"And it is a testament to my great compassion that I have not already disowned you," her mother retorted with an imperious sniff. But Anna noticed that her mother's voice trembled over the words, and she was moved to compassion.

She understood her mother's plight. She was a sick old woman with no-one left in the world save her daughter. If she abandoned her in this condition simply because their religious convictions could not be reconciled, Anna felt she would be no better than those who persecuted reformists. She couldn't coerce her mother into doing what she had no desire to do, and yet—

"If Henry and I marry, I can take you to live with me, Mama," she said, trying a different approach. "We can have a real home again. A real family."

Frau Adlischweiler whipped around with surprising force, pointing a finger at Anna's chest. "You will not marry that man while I live and breathe," she said quietly. "And I will brook no defiance from you on this matter either."

Anna felt her own anger surge. "I am not a child, Mother," she ground out. "I am 23 years old. I have gained my majority. I can—"

"You are *my* child," her mother screeched with more vigour than Anna had imagined she possessed. "And you will not marry a heretic!"

Molten anger seethed within Anna as she glared at her mother. They glowered at one another like warriors in battle, neither willing to back down. Finally, Anna stepped back, let out a frustrated growl, and stormed out of the room.

When Henry arrived later that day, Anna recounted the episode in bitter detail. "What are we going to do?" she sobbed, burying her face in his shoulder.

Henry was silent for a moment as he patted her back, then he sighed. "We could simply disregard her wishes and marry."

Anna snapped upright. "What?"

"We are at an impasse," he said, leaning against the stone wall at his back. "Your mother hates me because of my faith. I am not prepared to recant my views, and she is not prepared to recant hers. She will never give us her blessing, so it seems to me that our best option is to go ahead and marry."

"Henry!" Anna exclaimed. "I can't just abandon my mother!"

Henry took her hand. "What else can we do, *liebchen*? You offered her a place in our home but she refused." He paused, brow furrowed in thought. "We can hire a maid to care for her after you're gone, so she won't be alone. And we can visit her here. What other option do we have?"

Anna was silent. She clutched the edge of the bench they sat upon, searching his face. Finally, she spoke. "I can't marry you, Henry," she said softly.

His face paled and he swallowed hard. "What do you mean?"

Anna buried her face in her hands, struggling to retain her composure, before raising her head to look him in the eye. "I cannot defy my mother. I am all she has. If we marry, she will never see me again. And she needs me, though she is too proud to admit it. She cannot survive alone. She will die in this convent—alone. I can't do that to her."

Henry stared at her in bitter realisation. "Must we truly allow ourselves to be held hostage by an angry old woman?"

Anna smiled sadly, reaching out to take his hand in hers. "No," she said. "I must make a hard choice for the sake of someone I love. And so must you." Tears welled in her eyes, but she blinked them back. "I can't abandon her, Henry," she choked out in a whisper. "I need to care for her. That is not only my duty as a daughter, but also the work God has given me to do in this season of my life. I cannot turn my back on that."

Henry watched her for a long moment, lips pursed in thought, then he nodded. Reaching forward, he gathered her in his arms and pressed his cheek against the crown of her head.

"I'll wait," he said, exhaling a long breath. "For as long as it takes, Anna, I'll wait."

Birmenstorf, Switzerland
August 17, 1529

Anna's wedding day dawned bittersweet. When she had begun this journey so long ago, she had often wondered if she would ever marry Henry. There were times when she was racked with guilt and longing in equal measure. She wanted to enter Henry's world and help him spread the gospel, but she felt tethered to her ailing mother's side by an unseen hand. She was a prisoner yearning for the day of her release but dreading it all the same, for she would only gain her freedom when her mother breathed her last.

Henry remained faithful and steadfast, going so far as to write her a small book about the biblical expectations placed upon a woman. She hadn't known whether to laugh or cry or throw the book at his head when she received it, so she settled for pasting on a prim expression and thanking him prettily for his pains.

Now, like Jacob of old who waited patiently for his bride, Henry Bullinger had finally received leave to claim his. Fortunately for Henry, he had not had to wait seven years for Anna; nor did she have any sisters to thwart his long-held plans. Anna giggled at these thoughts as she smoothed her simple dress in the small anteroom at the back of the church where they were to wed.

Her mother had passed peacefully six weeks ago, and Anna had waited long enough to see to the burial, pack up her belongings and settle her mother's estate before sending word to Henry that she was ready to marry him.

A swift rap on the door preceded Henry's entrance. They grinned when they saw each other, and Henry bowed deeply.

"Well, look at you, Fräulein Adlischweiler," he said, offering her a small bouquet of wildflowers. "As pretty as a picture."

"Oh, Henry, they're beautiful," she replied, taking them from him with a curtsey.

"Ready to become Frau Bullinger?" he asked.

"As ready as I will ever be."

She tucked her hand into the crook of his proffered arm, and her smiled softened as she gazed up at him. "Thank you for waiting for me, Henry."

His own smile turned tender as he laid a hand over hers. "You were worth every moment, *liebchen*," he said softly. "Worth every moment."

Anna Bullinger (neé Adlischweiler) was born around 1504. Historical sources differ regarding her admittance to the convent. While some say that she was donated to the Ottenbach Convent in Zurich following her father's death, when she was about eight years old, others propose she entered the convent later in life, around 1523. Her mother, who had been ill for much of Anna's life, joined the convent sometime after Anna entered it, to be cared for as an invalid.

In 1522, the Zurich city council ordered Ulrich Zwingli to preach to the nuns at the convent, and he and Leo Juda took over their spiritual care when the council forbade the Dominican monks who had previously engaged in this work to enter the convent. In 1527, Juda took Henry Bullinger with him to the convent. He was quickly smitten with Anna and his letter of proposal is the oldest surviving love letter from a reformer, offering a glimpse into early Reformation courtship. Anna's response is also enlightening. Though she initially accepted his proposal, she later refused it, to care for her ailing mother who was bitterly opposed to the match between Bullinger and her daughter.

Despite these setbacks, Anna and Henry were married six weeks after Anna's mother's death. The Bullingers' marriage was happy and they had 11 children. Henry was one of the leading proponents of the Swiss Reformation and had numerous responsibilities. Their home was a gathering place for other reformers and scholars and a refuge for many who were persecuted for their faith, including Zwingli's widow and children. In 1546, Henry fell ill with the plague. Anna nursed him to recovery; however, she subsequently contracted the illness and died on September 25, 1546. Henry outlived Anna by 11 years but chose not to remarry.

9

Argula von Grumbach

THE ADVOCATE

Bavaria, Germany
1523

When Arsacius Seehofer awoke that morning, all was right in his world. But when he went to bed that night, he was in jail.

The trouble began with his morning lectures. He was a member of the Faculty of Theology at the University of Ingolstadt at just 18 years old—a fact that made him preen. He could hardly believe they allowed him to conduct lectures. *Him!* A humble scholar so vastly inferior to the likes of his esteemed mentor Philip Melanchthon. Yet here he was, tasked with the spiritual instruction of young men like himself. He relished the work.

That morning, he decided to make a stand—to be as daring as Luther—by revealing more of his newfound beliefs. He presented a rousing lecture on the doctrine of justification by faith, directly from Scripture. When he left the lecture hall, he could still picture the awestruck faces of his pupils. He was pleased—so thoroughly pleased that he failed to notice the contingent of guards following him. So thoroughly preoccupied with his plans to further the Reformation at Ingolstadt that he didn't realise they had come for him until they were right there, jostling him and demanding that he open his room for them.

"Why?" he sputtered, as a fissure of dread slithered across his skin and pebbled his flesh.

"We have been ordered to search your rooms," a guard said, his face stoic and implacable.

"By whom?" Arsacius demanded, feigning outrage while he desperately tried to remember where he had put his stack of Lutheran pamphlets. Had he replaced them in their hiding place beneath his mattress or were they still lying on his desk?

"By the rector," a second guard sneered, shoving Arsacius out of the way and barrelling towards the door to his small chamber.

"How dare you!" Arsacius shouted, struggling to get ahead of the guard and bar the door. "You have no right—"

His words were cut off as the door gave way, and they both tumbled into the room. Arsacius was wrestled away by a bruising pair of hands and held steady while the guards searched his room. He noted, with detached relief, that the pamphlets were not on his desk. However, the relief was short-lived. When one of the guards hoisted his thin mattress, he found a cache of small booklets lying on the ropes that threaded the frame beneath.

"Well, well," said the guard, with a mocking smile. "What do we have here, Professor?"

Arsacius tilted his chin defiantly, even as he felt the blood rush from his face to pool like ice in his belly. The guard bent over, picked up a pamphlet and pretended to read it.

"A little forbidden reading?" he asked smugly, though it seemed he could not read the cursive script scrawled across the cover.

Arsacius, however, could read. He knew that the cover proclaimed, *The Babylonian Captivity of the Church* by Martin Luther. He also knew that he was in deep, deep trouble.

Argula von Grumbach prided herself on her ability to act like a lady. She was, after all, part of the Bavarian nobility, though somewhat impoverished due to circumstances beyond her control—warring dukes and greedy relatives. And she had been raised in the household of the dowager Duchess of Bavaria. Yet, that morning, she was so completely enraged that she forgot all about being ladylike as she stormed into her husband's study.

Friedrich was seated behind a large desk, quill in hand, scribbling away as though his life depended on it.

"Have you heard what they have done to Arsacius Seehofer?" she demanded, jolting to a halt before him, hands fisted on hips enlarged by her voluminous dress.

Friedrich did not raise his head or stop his scratching, which infuriated Argula more. She was just opening her mouth to speak again, when he said, without looking up, "No, I haven't heard, but I am sure you have come to tell me." He glanced at her then, his expression communicating a familiar mixture of emotions—amusement, exasperation, grim resignation. None of it the staunch support she was hoping to see, but she would take what little of his attention she could get.

"They have compelled him, on pain of imprisonment and death, to recant his faith," she said, sitting on the stool positioned directly before him.

He paused, head tilted, as he considered this information. "Who has?" he asked.

"The Faculty of Theology at the University of Ingolstadt," Argula snapped.

Friedrich shrugged, then resumed his writing. "Isn't Dr Eck there?" he asked casually.

Argula stared at the top of his head. "Dr Eck?" she replied, feigning ignorance.

Friedrich tipped his face towards her and raised an accusatory eyebrow. "Dr Eck," he repeated. "The famous papal scholar who debated against Luther."

"Ah, *that* Dr Eck," she hedged peevishly, as her husband's glare bored into her like an awl. She shrugged. "Yes, I suppose he is."

"And is Seehofer one of Luther's disciples?" Friedrich pressed, eyes narrowed.

"Melanchthon's," Argula snapped, crossing her arms over her chest. She knew full well that to follow one was to follow the other, though she was not about to admit it.

"And has Seehofer been teaching Melanchthon's views at the university?"

Argula exhaled an exasperated sigh, "Yes, but—"

"Then why are you surprised that they have arrested him?" Friedrich asked incredulously. "If he insists on doing something so foolish, then it is little wonder he has to pay for his stupidity."

"But he has done nothing wrong!" Argula exclaimed, shooting off her stool like a cork loosed from a bottle. "He has simply preached the truth as it is revealed in Scripture. Why must he pay for that?"

"Because he lives in a world that is regulated by the pope, the church and the Duke of Bavaria. Scripture has nothing to do with it."

"How can you say that?" she demanded, appalled. "Scripture is the rule of our faith."

Friedrich sighed, laid down his pen and pinched the bridge of his nose. "Argula," he began, in a tone she knew well. He was going to lecture her on propriety. She wanted to tear her hair out in frustration, but she forced herself to remain motionless. "Even if what they have done to him is unconscionable, it is not our concern. First, because he is a heretic if he follows Luther, and second, because we cannot afford to displease the Duke of Bavaria in any way. My livelihood is in his gift. If he dismisses me, we will not have food on our table or a roof over our heads."

"So we must cower like mice while injustice is being perpetrated?" she demanded.

"No, we must think of ourselves and our children first." Friedrich glared a warning at her. "Leave this matter. If Seehofer was foolish enough to be caught teaching Luther's heresy, then he deserves to bear the consequences of his actions."

"Even if those consequences are unjust? Even if those consequences violate the most fundamental right he possesses as a human being?"

"And what right is that?" he asked dryly, raising an eyebrow.

"The right to a free conscience. The right to worship God as Scripture dictates."

"None of us have the luxury of that right!" he snapped.

"Then we must fight for it!" she retorted.

Friedrich's expression took on the likeness of a thundercloud, dark and foreboding. "Leave this," he said, firmly. "It is not your concern."

Argula's mouth tightened, and she glared at him with rising defiance. "We will see about that," she barked, before turning on her heel and leaving as turbulently as she had come.

That night, when the children were in bed and she was alone in her room, Argula decided—against all good sense and her husband's repeated warnings—that she could not remain silent. If her only recourse was to use her words in this battle, then she would wield them as surely as a knight wielded his sword. She fetched a fresh sheet of paper, sharpened her quill, opened an ampule of ink and began to write.

> To the honourable Rector and all the Faculty at the University of Ingolstadt,
>
> How in God's name can you and your university expect to prevail when you deploy such violence against the Word of God? When you force someone to hold the Holy Gospel in their hands for the very purpose of denying it as you did in the case of Arsacius Seehofer?
>
> Yes, when I reflect on this, my heart and all my limbs tremble. What do Luther and Melanchthon teach save the Word of God?

> You condemned them without refuting them. Did Christ teach you so? Show me where it is written! Neither the pope, nor the kaiser, nor the princes have any authority over the Word of God.

Her words poured from her quill in a hot flourish, searing their way across the page. She would not be silent. Not when she had the power to advocate on behalf of this wronged young man. Yes, he had recanted, but what of it? God was gracious, and perhaps if Arsacius perceived that someone was for him—on his side—he might yet choose to make a stand for the right.

> The Lord will forgive Arsacius as he forgave Peter when he denied his Master. Great good will yet come from this young man. I send you not a woman's ranting but the Word of God. I write as a member of the Church of Christ against which the gates of hell shall not prevail, as they will against the Church of Rome.

She signed her missive with a flourish, then sat back with a satisfied smile. She might be disdained as a woman, but she was not weak. She could use her voice to advocate.

Arsacius learned how fickle life can be in the space of a few short hours. He also learned how fickle *he* could be given the right circumstances. He had been tried three times, and like Peter in the courtyard of Caiaphas, he had denied his Lord each time.

He couldn't comprehend it. He had been sure of his unfailing loyalty to Christ—but then they had threatened him with the stake. That was his undoing, for he could not bear the thought of his flesh bubbling in the flames.

They had asked him to stand before the entire faculty, place his hand upon a Bible—a *Bible* of all things—and recant his faith. He had done so, weeping like the cowardly fool he was. Then he had been forced to thank them—*thank them!*—for their leniency, before being transported here, to a godforsaken cloister on the edge of the earth, where he had been left to rot.

During the chaos of the past weeks, he had heard of a woman somewhere in Bavaria who had taken up his cause. She had written to the university, condemning their behaviour in forcing him to recant. The news had shaken him anew, made him wonder—if she was brave enough to defend him, why on earth had he not been brave enough to defend himself?

He had been a fool, momentarily blinded by his fear. Now, seething with despair, all he longed for was an opportunity to make a different choice.

Argula's letter raised a firestorm of anger. She was called every vile name under the sun. The Duke of Bavaria called Friedrich into his personal chambers and told him to bring his wife to heel.

"Cut off her fingers to prevent her taking up a quill or strangle her if you must, but for heaven's sake, shut her up!" he had roared. He had then dismissed Friedrich from his employ.

When her husband informed her of the consequences of her actions that evening, Argula wondered if he really would cut off her fingers or strangle her. He did neither. He simply went to bed and spent the next several weeks stewing in a cauldron of resentment and rage.

They were forced to leave their home. Find other employment. Her children suffered. Her husband hated her. Her family wished her dead. Yet for all that, Argula could not bring herself to regret her actions. If she had not spoken on behalf of that young man, then who on earth would have? None of the men in Christendom seemed to care enough to say a word.

As time passed, she found that she was not entirely alone. Luther corresponded with her frequently, encouraging her. She was given an audience with the Count of the Palatinate and invited to speak at the Diet of Augsburg as a special guest. She even found her letter printed and distributed throughout Bavaria. But perhaps the most encouraging news of all came when she heard that Arsacius Seehofer had managed to escape the cloister where he had been imprisoned. The last anyone had heard of him, he had been travelling on foot, preaching the gospel to anyone willing to listen.

Argula von Grumbach (née von Stauff) was born in Bavaria in 1492. She was influenced by the writings of Martin Luther in the early 1520s and jumped into the fray of the Reformation when she wrote her impassioned letter defending Arsacius Seehofer in 1523, for which she was condemned and persecuted. The historical record mentions her again in 1563, when she was imprisoned by the Duke of Bavaria for circulating books contrary to the Catholic religion and inviting parishioners to Protestant church services in her home. She was released on compassionate grounds because of her advanced age and died shortly thereafter. Argula von Grumbach was the Reformation's first published female writer.

10

Wibrandis Rosenblatt

A LIGHT IN THE WINDOW

Martinskirche Parsonage, Basel, Switzerland
Autumn, 1526

John Oecolampadius was accustomed to troublesome friends, but he liked them better when they weren't underfoot. At present, his patience was being sorely tested by a house guest who was both a beloved friend and a meddlesome pest. His presence had prompted John to pray most fervently for the fruits of the Spirit.

"Marriage is an honourable state, especially for a Christian pastor," urged Wolfgang Capito. He had been pontificating on the subject for the entirety of their walk from the university to John's small home behind St Martin's Church.

"I don't need a wife," John repeated for what seemed like the tenth time in as many minutes, as he unlocked the door to the small parsonage and passed into the foyer.

"I really think you do," Wolfgang countered as he shrugged off his cloak, took off his cap and hung them both on a peg.

John followed suit, glaring at him all the while.

"What?" Wolfgang protested with wide-eyed innocence. "Every man needs a wife. The Lord Himself told us it is not good that a man should be alone."

"Oh, for heaven's sake," John muttered.

In the tiny kitchen at the back of the house, Wolfgang sank down onto a stool at the weathered table.

"You only want me to find a wife because you have found one," John grumbled, rummaging in a cupboard for bread and cheese.

"I don't deny that," Wolfgang agreed cheerfully. "Like you, I once believed myself called to celibacy—"

"You were a Catholic priest," John muttered, setting a loaf of bread and a hunk of cheese on the table before taking his own seat.

"Yes, I was a Catholic priest. But even after I embraced reform, I still believed that celibacy was my calling until my friends pressed me to consider marriage."

"I don't need friends like that," John responded sullenly, reaching for the bread. "I'd rather have a dozen enemies instead."

Wolfgang grinned, watching as John sliced the bread and carved off a considerable slice of cheese. John passed the knife to Wolfgang and began eating his meal.

"Listen, even my wife didn't want to get married until her brothers convinced her that I was a reasonably good bet."

John rolled his eyes. "What is your point?" he ground out, biting into his bread and cheese with exaggerated gusto.

"All I'm saying is that sometimes we need friends to give us a push in the right direction."

"I am a contented bachelor!" John exclaimed. "Pushing me into marriage is like pushing me into the path of a runaway carriage."

"What about your housekeeper?" Wolfgang asked, ignoring John's outburst. "And can I get something to drink?"

Sighing, John set his bread on the table and rose to rustle about for a jug. "I'm certain she left a jug of something or other around here somewhere," he muttered.

Wolfgang paused, watching John until he located a brown jug, which he held up in triumph.

"So, what about your housekeeper?" he pressed.

Groaning, John buried his head in his free hand. Drawing in a steadying breath, he willed his temper to calm before addressing Wolfgang.

"Look," he began with exaggerated patience, "I appreciate your concern, but it's no use." He set the jug down on the table between them. "Besides, women who believe as I do are as rare as hen's teeth."

"Your housekeeper believes as you do," Wolfgang pointed out, as persistent as a dog with a bone.

"I can't stand her!" John blurted out in exasperation. He ran a hand through his hair. "I wouldn't for a moment consider marrying her, but I can't get rid of her either." He nodded towards the jug. "Go on, then," he said, desperate to change the subject. "I thought you said you wanted something to drink."

Wolfgang nodded gravely, looking for all the world as if he were taking John's words to heart. Then he looked up. "Either way, I think you need a wife."

John glowered at him. "I just told you—"

Wolfgang held up a placating hand. "If for no other reason than to teach you to use plates and mugs when you serve your guests."

Basel, Switzerland
March, 1528

"Are you sure you know what you're doing?" Elsa demanded, eyeing Wibrandis as she packed her small trunk. "He's so old!"

Wibrandis glowered at her friend, who was bouncing Wibrandis's small daughter against her shoulder, attempting to rock her to sleep.

"He's a decent man who's willing to marry a newly widowed woman with a child. I can't afford to be picky."

Elsa sighed dramatically, pacing the small room as she patted the baby's back. "He's gaunt and pale, and have you *seen* his beard?"

"Oh, for heaven's sake, I'm not marrying his beard," Wibrandis muttered, tossing a folded gown into the trunk, then turning to pick up another small pile of clothes.

"You could very well be marrying his beard," Elsa said darkly. "Who knows if he will expect you to trim it for him!"

"Elsa!" Wibrandis exclaimed, startling the baby, who immediately began to wail. Exhaling a calming breath, Wibrandis sank down onto the bed and buried her face in her hands. "I have nowhere else to go," she whispered. "It's not as if I have a dozen suitors lining up outside my door, and pride won't pay the rent."

Elsa sank onto a stool, cradling the baby's small head in her palm. "But John Oecolampadius?" she asked dubiously. "The man is just so . . . old."

Wibrandis shook her head, a small smirk tugging on the corners of her lips. "Apart from the fact that he is older than I am," she said, "he is one of the leading scholars of Basel, a brilliant theologian, a leader of the Reformation, and well able to provide for me and Little Wibrandis." Wibrandis nodded towards her small namesake who had fallen asleep, mouth gaping wide, on Elsa's shoulder.

Elsa considered her words. "But will you be happy?" she finally asked.

"Happiness is a choice," Wibrandis said softly. Then she sighed. "He is a good man, Elsa. Decent, kind and hardworking. He isn't going to drink at the tavern every night and come home to beat me. Nor is he going to be miserly and deprive me of food and clothing. I am too practical to wonder if he will write me long love letters or if he will even love me at all. He will provide for me. He will treat me well. And I will be able to contribute to his ministry. What more could I want?"

Elsa twisted her lips in thought, then sighed. "You're right," she finally said. "But let us hope for both your sakes that he knows how to trim his own beard."

Martinskirche Parsonage, Basel, Switzerland
February, 1529

All of Basel was in an uproar and John was at the centre of the raging storm. He had been working tirelessly to advance reform in Basel, but the city officials were reluctant and suspicious by turns. Finally, he had turned to the guilds, hoping that their support would help him influence more people. The result was bittersweet. He did not care for rioting mobs. He was a man who tended to peace, yet the citizens of Basel, embracing reform, had taken to the streets in a wave of destruction.

As he trudged home, wrestling within himself, John felt weighed down with discouragement and doubt. But when he turned down the small lane leading to the parsonage, his eyes fastened on a candle in the front window of his home, which was flickering valiantly against the encroaching darkness. His heart leapt in his chest as he realised that Wibrandis had left a candle in the window for him, to light his way home after dark.

His picked up his pace, crunching down the gravel path until he came to his door. He swung it open and was immediately greeted by the mewling cries of an infant. Slipping out of his hat and cloak, he rushed to the kitchen where he found his wife standing over the hearth, stirring a pot of stew with one hand and cradling their squalling son in the other. Little Wibrandis was clinging to her skirts, whining her discontent at her mother's distraction. When he entered, all three of them turned towards him, and he felt a strange warmth slither through his chest.

"Papa!" Little Wibrandis cried, releasing her mother's skirts and toddling towards him.

Wibrandis smiled. "You're home," she said, relief washing over her weary face.

John picked up his small daughter, swinging her in the air and eliciting a volley of delighted giggles, before kissing his wife on the cheek.

"I am home," he agreed.

He set Little Wibrandis down with the instruction to sit on her small stool at the table. Then he scooped up the red-faced Eusebius, settling him against his shoulder and pacing with him. The baby settled, the toddler found a plate and spoon to entertain herself with, and Wibrandis brought the steaming stew and fresh bread to the table.

After dinner, John led his family in worship—singing a psalm and reading a short portion of Scripture—before tucking Little Wibrandis into her trundle bed. When he finally sat down in his chair before the hearth, the troubles of the day seemed a world away, swallowed by the simple joys of being a husband and father.

"How was it today?" Wibrandis asked, coming to sit beside him, a basket of mending in her hands.

He rubbed his face wearily. "I don't know if I should rejoice at the progress we're making or weep at the violence of that progress."

"They have been looting churches?" Wibrandis asked quietly, her nimble fingers plying a needle over a tear in one of his shirts.

John watched her hands work, binding the ripped material with sturdy thread. "I wish the truth could take hold without strife," he said softly.

Wibrandis looked at him with sympathy and compassion. "We live in a world caught between the forces of good and evil. While the devil is alive, perfect peace will always elude us."

"I do not care for the violence," John said.

"No," Wibrandis agreed, "but if the people want reform and the city authorities resist them, I can understand their desire to force the issue."

John sank back in this chair, closing his eyes with a weary sigh. "It looks like they will abolish the mass in Basel."

"Oh, John!" Wibrandis exclaimed. "That is an answer to prayer."

John turned to look at her and smiled. "It is," he agreed. "When all this began, I didn't think we would live to see the people of Basel rally to progress the cause of reform."

Wibrandis reached her hand towards his and he clasped it, squeezing affectionately. "Then let us focus on our victories and leave our defeats in God's hands," she said with a gentle smile.

October, 1530

Wibrandis bustled about her small kitchen in a frenzy, stirring the simmering stew, checking the bread in the oven and trying to make sure the children didn't get trampled or burned. Elsa watched her from the table where she was setting out plates, utensils and a platter of cheese.

"If you don't stop scurrying about like that, you'll be too exhausted to greet your guests," she said severely, bending to scoop little Eusebius from the floor and kiss his fat cheeks. "He's grown." She planted another kiss on his cheek as he squirmed to be set down.

Wibrandis gave her son a fond smile and nodded, resting a hand on her expanding belly. "He's a handful."

"Where's John?" Elsa asked, going to the oven to check on the bread.

"Out in the street watching for the pastors. He's afraid they'll take a wrong turn."

Elsa rolled her eyes, wrapped her apron around her hand and took the bread out of the oven with a wooden paddle. "How anyone could miss St Martin's Church is beyond me," she muttered.

Wibrandis gave the stew another stir. "He is understandably excited."

Elsa set the bread on the table. "I would be too," she conceded. "Imagine, the Waldenses coming to visit!"

Wibrandis grinned as she hefted the stew pot, waddling over to set it on the table with a loud thump. "Imagine hosting them for a few weeks," she countered, cheeks flushed with a combination of exertion and trepidation. "Did you ever imagine, when you were lecturing me about trimming John's beard, that I would be hosting a delegation from one of Christendom's most ancient and faithful churches?"

Elsa eyed her critically then shrugged. "I didn't doubt that marrying John Oecolampadius would have *some* advantages," she said airily. "I was just concerned about his aging frame and unruly facial hair."

Wibrandis burst out laughing. "Well, you can rest assured that neither his aging frame nor his facial hair have detracted from his charms—chief of which is his love for God's cause."

Elsa cracked a reluctant smile. "But tell me truly, Wibrandis. Are you happy? Are you glad you married him?"

Wibrandis walked over to her friend and flung an arm around her shoulders. "I am happy," she confirmed. "I am doing the work God has called me to do." She squeezed Elsa's arm. "I am not a preacher or a teacher or a theologian, but I am advancing the cause of reform as surely as any of them are, and I couldn't ask for a higher calling than that."

Wibrandis Rosenblatt was born in 1504 in Basel. She outlived four husbands—Ludwig Keller, John Oecolampadius, Wolfgang Capito (who had encouraged Oecolampadius to marry Wibrandis) and Martin Bucer—men remembered for their work as scholars and leaders of the Reformation in Basel and Strasbourg. Wibrandis is representative of a new group of women who emerged at the time of the Reformation— women who served God as minister's wives—as Protestant ministers were not required to be celibate. At the time of her marriage to John Oecolampadius, Wibrandis was 24 and he 45. As she did with her other husbands, Wibrandis played both a significant role in supporting John's ministry and in ministering in her own right, including hosting a delegation of Waldensian Christians, a persecuted group, who came to confer with Oecolampadius and Ulrich Zwingli. When Wibrandis succumbed to the plague that swept through Basel in 1564, she was laid to rest beside her second husband, John Oecolampadius.

11

Margaret of Navarre

A Shelter in the Time of Storm

The Palace of the Louvre, Paris, France
October, 1533

Reformists always managed to get into trouble, and it seemed to Margaret of Navarre that they didn't try very hard to avoid it either. She wished they would, for it would spare her the inconvenience of grovelling before her brother Francis, the King of France.

"Have you heard what your beloved miscreants have done this time?" he asked without preamble as she was ushered into his privy chamber. He dismissed his gentlemen with a flick of his wrist, watching Margaret like a cat observes a bird it would like to devour.

Margaret held his stare with characteristic calm, determined to emerge victorious from this tussle. When the room was empty, Francis turned his back on her and wandered over to an ornate golden chair situated beside a window overlooking the Seine. "Well?" he prompted, when the silence between them grew prolonged.

"I don't know—" Margaret began, but he cut her off with an impatient snort.

"Don't add insult to injury by lying to me," he snapped. "I know you let them off with nothing more than a slap on the wrist."

Margaret sighed and came to sit beside him. "Fine," she admitted. "I heard about what happened, but I took care of the problem without dragging you into the mess."

"Oh, don't pretend you were being considerate of me," he groused. "You didn't involve me because you wanted to protect your little reformists."

It occurred to Margaret that there might be a disparity between their understanding of the situation. Precisely how much did her brother know?

"What have you heard?" she finally asked.

"That two artisans of Alençon, closet reformists who were overtaken by a sudden urge to display their zeal, stole statues of saints from the local church and hung them upside-down from a gutter." Francis watched her with barely leashed fury. "Is that an accurate summation of events?"

Margaret blanched. "Yes," she admitted meekly.

"Imagine my surprise," Francis continued, "when I was informed of these events by a messenger from the Parlement and not my own sister, who happens to be the sovereign of the Duchy of Alençon!" He exploded from his chair like a cannonball, moving to pace before the fireplace that dominated a wall of his opulent chamber.

"I told you—" Margaret began.

"Oh, spare me the platitudes. Let us speak plainly to one another. I pray we are able to at least have that between us."

Margaret bolted to her feet and rushed to clasp his hands. "Francis," she said softly, "I did not mean to lie to you."

She and Francis were close. Closer than any siblings Margaret had ever met. But on one point—religious conviction—their paths had begun to increasingly diverge. Margaret squeezed her brother's hands. She loved him dearly, yet she couldn't countenance seeing innocent men and women being burnt for their faith.

"I thought that issuing them with a fine was sufficient punishment for their crimes."

Francis's jaw hardened. "On that point, I beg to differ." Gently, he extricated his hands from her grasp and returned to his chair. Sinking into it, he leaned back, settled his elbows on the arms and steepled his fingers before him. "You need not worry though," he said smoothly. "I have settled the matter as I saw fit."

Margaret felt a rush of panic. "What have you done?" she whispered.

Francis looked away from her for a moment, then turned to glare at her defiantly. "I have ordered them to be burned for their insolence." He pointed a finger at her. "Let this be a lesson, Margaret. I am willing to spare your beloved reformers when the situation warrants, but this incident is an example of what I will not tolerate."

John du Bellay, Bishop of Paris, appreciated the fine art of a delicate balance. He enjoyed it in the flavours of his food, the subtle nuances of his spiced drinks and even in the clothes he wore. However, when maintaining a delicate balance spilled over into matters of life and death, he found it too tedious for his taste.

He entered the presence chamber of the king's sister, wondering how he could navigate the situation before him without getting himself or anyone else killed.

"Ah, Bishop," Margaret's dulcet voice drew him out of his ruminations.

He bowed, then offered her a wry smile. "I have come to seek your counsel, Your Highness."

"And I have been thinking of sending you a message," she said with a similar smile, "for I am desperately in need of yours, Your Grace."

"Then we are both in luck."

"That we are," Margaret agreed. She motioned for John to join her in a quiet alcove of the vast room. It was public enough for propriety, yet secluded enough to give them a modicum of privacy.

"What news?" she began, her whisper urgent.

John's eyebrows rose at her tone. "What news have you?" he asked, eyeing her. "Your tone tells me something is amiss."

Margaret nodded slowly. "I have had an audience with my brother," she began, then relayed the conversation to him.

John felt the blood rushing from his face as he contemplated the severity and swiftness of the king's actions. "He has no patience for bold displays of zeal then," he breathed.

"No," Margaret replied, studying him. "Do you bring news of an impending display of that nature?"

John rubbed his forehead. "I'm afraid I do," he confirmed. "Nicholas Cop wishes to give an incendiary speech to the faculty and students at his inaugural address as Rector of the University of Paris."

Margaret's eyebrows rose.

John sighed and pinched the bridge of his nose. "It was Calvin's idea. He has even gone so far as to write the speech for Cop."

Margaret stared at him, wide-eyed. "By incendiary, I presume you mean he wishes to preach the gospel?" she clarified.

John nodded.

"God have mercy upon us all," she breathed.

"That is precisely what I have been praying since I heard of it," John agreed grimly.

"Have they forgotten what happened to me when I opened the Louvre and allowed the gospel to be preached here?" Margaret asked suddenly. "Have they forgotten how the Faculty of Theology at the University of Paris called for my arrest?" She shook her head as she relived the memory. Her brother had arrived to save her as he always did. But her brother's patience had limits, as she had just seen.

"No-one has forgotten that, Your Highness," John assured her wryly.

"I cannot intercede on their behalf if the worst should happen," she said, wanting the bishop to understand how desperately limited she was. "My brother is angry about the affair in Alençon."

Margaret glanced at John to see if he knew what she referred to and he offered her grim nod of affirmation.

"No-one suspects what is afoot?" she asked.

John shook his head. "No. No-one knows what they are planning. I just wanted you to be forewarned should the worst happen."

Margaret nodded slowly. "If the worst happens, I am sure God will give us the wisdom to navigate it. Until then, let us wait. Keep me informed."

John bowed and left the room. Everyone in their small network of reformists had a role, like cogs in a well-oiled machine—some parts sturdier, some parts more delicate, but all working in concert towards a single goal. Calvin would write the speech, Cop would deliver it, and John would work with the Queen of Navarre to ensure they both lived to see another day.

Paris, France
November, 1533

The urgent rapping on her chamber door woke Margaret from a sound sleep. She blinked, then sat up with a gasp. She scrambled out of bed, snatching up her robe, before scurrying to the hearth to light a candle.

"Who is it?" she called, walking to the door of her privy chamber. Her heart was hammering in her chest, her breathing shallow. A knock in the small hours of the night never boded well.

"Your Highness, a messenger has just brought a letter," one of her maids called through the heavy wood.

Margaret opened the door and reached for the folded parchment. "Who was it?" she asked, handing her candle to the maid so she could tear open the seal.

"I don't know," the maid said, holding the candle over the sheet of paper so Margaret could read. The hastily scrawled words conveyed a grave message.

"Summon the Bishop of Paris at once," she said urgently to her wide-eyed maid as she turned back into her room. "Tell him to meet me in my presence chamber without delay."

When John strode into Margaret's presence chamber just before dawn, his face was set in grim lines.

"You have heard," Margaret stated without preamble.

He nodded. "A messenger from the Parlement informed me, requesting my presence at the proceedings."

Margaret drew in a breath.

"Are you privy to information I do not have?" he asked her.

Margaret considered this. "I do not believe so. I was only warned by an anonymous messenger that Nicholas Cop is to be summoned this morning to appear before the Parlement of Paris."

Nicholas Cop had used his inaugural address at the University of Paris to preach the gospel, just as John had warned he was planning to do. He had challenged the faculty and created as big an uproar as Margaret had when she had dared to preach the gospel from the Louvre this past summer. Paris was in turmoil.

"It is as we feared," John said, pursing his lips. "The Faculty of Theology wants him burned. The message I received informed me that they plan to lure him to the Palais du Justice under the pretence of a hearing, only to arrest him when he enters the building, imprison him and then burn him."

Margaret clenched her teeth in fury. "They will not get away with it," she said, curling her small hands into fists. "I will not allow them to sacrifice a good man just to satisfy their lust for blood."

"I couldn't agree more," John replied. "How do you propose to save him?"

Margaret narrowed her eyes at him with a smile. "I won't," she said softly, "but you will."

Nicholas Cop had an uneasy feeling about his meeting this morning. He was dressed in his robes of office and carrying the great seal of the University of Paris on his person. Surrounded by his retinue of servants, he moved through the streets of Paris with great pomp, looking like the important man he was, but his mind was whirling. He had seen enough heretics burn to fear for his life, but he tried to reassure himself that he had never seen the Rector of the University of Paris burned.

That could be because you're the first Rector to ever preach a reformist sermon from the university pulpit, he pointed out to himself.

He firmly suppressed this thought. No. They might question him, but they would not lay a finger upon him. He had immunity. He was exempt from being tried as a heretic.

Unless the sermon went a step too far, his thoughts continued morbidly.

People gathered thickly about him as they always did when an important man or woman processed through the city. Some called out to him, others held out upturned palms, begging for money. Vendors threaded through their midst selling apples and sweets.

Suddenly, a man leapt out of the crowd in front of him. Gasping, Nicholas stepped back, ready to flee, but the man reached forward, grasped his shoulders and drew him into an embrace.

"The Parlement plans to arrest you as soon as you enter the Palais du Justice," the man whispered in his ear. "Escape into the crowd and meet me outside St Germain l'Auxerrois within the hour. I will help you escape." With that, he shoved Nicholas away, ducked his head and melted into the crowd.

Nicholas gaped after him, sweat pouring down his back, his heart whirring like a trapped moth in his chest. His servant approached him, concern marring his brow.

"Rector—" the servant began, stretching out his hand to assist him.

Nicholas waved him away, his mind clicking through one plan after another as he desperately tried to think of an escape. In the end, he chose the simplest option.

Turning, he plunged into the crowd, threading his way through the press of bodies. People shouted, grabbing at his clothes. A woman cried out as he crashed into her; someone shoved a hand into his face. He pushed away from them all, weaving, running, until he entered a small dark alley.

He heard the thud of footsteps behind him—surely his servants coming to see if he had lost his mind. Perhaps even guards from the Parlement who had been dispatched to seize him. He shook his head at that thought—no, too soon. They would have heard nothing of his escape yet.

Working quickly, he shed his doctoral cap and his heavy robes until he wore nothing but his hose and shirt. Then, without hesitation, he turned on his heel and ran.

John du Bellay had thought his troubles were at an end after he orchestrated the escape of Nicholas Cop at the queen's request. Cop had been smuggled to Geneva, where he was secure from the threat of persecution. The news of Cop's arrival in Switzerland had convinced him that all was well and that he could finally return to his duties as the Bishop of Paris. Alas, his peace was short lived.

This morning, he had received word that John Calvin was under suspicion for writing Cop's sermon. Du Bellay now stood before the Queen of Navarre once more, trying to navigate the treacherous waters ahead of them.

"I thought no-one knew?" Margaret asked in exasperation. "How are we to extricate Calvin so soon after dealing with Cop? We are both under suspicion already."

John expelled a weary breath. He understood her frustration. For the past decade, she had been constantly battling attempts by the ecclesiastical authorities to suppress the Reformation in France. She had won more battles than she had lost, but it was an exhausting business to keep fighting.

"The royal chancellor has someone watching him," he finally said, choosing to address her first question. "He suspects Calvin is behind it but can prove nothing. Or he has not been able to until now." John's mouth tightened.

Margaret rubbed her forehead. "I already told you; I cannot go to my brother."

John nodded. "I know, but perhaps we can think of another way?"

Pursing her lips, she drew a hand across her brow. "We cannot sacrifice Calvin," she said. "But under the current circumstances, direct intervention would be imprudent. Perhaps all we can do is warn him. We will have to pray that is enough."

John thought about this, then nodded. It was the best they could do. "I'll get word to his friends," he said, before bowing and turning to leave.

Collège de Forteret, University of Paris, France
December, 1533

John Calvin sat at his desk, gazing at the wall before him as he thought about the sermon he was writing. He turned to toss a small length of firewood into his grate and used the iron poker to push it further into the flames. At this moment, when he was warm and contented, without a care in the world, the door banged open, causing him to jump violently.

"What in heaven's name are you doing!" he exclaimed as he saw his friends Michel and Georges thunder into the room. They slammed the door behind them, grabbed his arms and propelled him towards the open window.

"Hurry," Michel urged, pushing against Calvin's resistance.

"What are you doing?" Calvin demanded, wrenching his arms away.

"The king's intendant is sending his men—" Michel began.

"As we speak," Georges interjected, jerking the sheets off Calvin's bed and grabbing the nightshirt off his bedpost for good measure. Calvin watched them, mouth gaping, trying to comprehend what was happening.

Michel stopped his frenzied action, paused in front of Calvin and slowly said, "They have discovered that you are the author of Cop's speech. The king's intendant has proof. He has already dispatched men to arrest you. They plan to take you to the Parlement, where you will be tried then burned for heresy. We have come to help you escape."

Calvin shut his mouth, opened it and shut it again.

"For heaven's sake, man, do not dither," Georges snapped.

He had tied Calvin's sheets, pillowcases and nightshirt together to fashion a makeshift rope. Calvin saw that one end was secured to the bed frame while the other dangled out the window.

"You must leave, John," Michel said, gripping his shoulders. "Now."

As the gravity of the situation sank in, Calvin sprang into action. He gathered nothing and asked no more questions. Instead, he swung one leg over the windowsill, clung to the makeshift rope and used it to lower himself to the ground. When his feet hit the cobbles, he turned to face his friends, lifting a fist in grateful solidarity.

"Godspeed," Michel said, keeping his voice low.

"Let us know when you are safe," Georges added.

Calvin nodded, turned on his heel and ran.

Margaret was seated beside the king when his chancellor came to report that yet another heretic had escaped Paris. She said nothing as he ranted about the reformist scourge that was infecting France, the impossibility of finding them all and the frustration of being thwarted at every turn. The king duly voiced his concern.

The chancellor eyed Margaret with suspicious fury, but she merely smiled at him benignantly. Silence seemed the appropriate response at a time like this. Besides, there was nothing to say. She had won this battle in the ongoing war. And by the grace of God, she meant to gain many, many more victories in the future. Her smile widened.

Margaret of Navarre was born in 1492. Her father, Charles, Count of Angoulême, was a Prince of the Blood, placing him directly in line to the throne of France. Her younger brother Francis became King Francis I of France. After Margaret accepted the doctrine of justification by faith, she wrote a book on the topic titled, The Mirror of the Sinful Soul. *In 1533, she opened the Louvre to the public in what would become the first Protestant evangelistic campaign in France. Some sources suggest that Margaret nurtured groups of reformers in Meaux in the early 1520s under the leadership of Jacques Lefèvre d'Étaples and William Briçonnet, and later in provinces such as Alençon, Berry and Aix. She is credited with interceding for and saving countless reformers from persecution and death, advocating for Waldensian Christians, a persecuted group in Toulouse, and promoting the growth of the Reformation through her books. Margaret died in 1549.*

12

Jeanne d'Albret

WITHIN GATES OF TRUTH

Château de Nerac, Navarre
Summer, 1535

Jeanne was kneeling beside her mother, listening to the lilting voice of Monsieur Farel, when the doors of the presence chamber burst open. There was a cacophony of sound—her father shouting, the rustling of her mother's gown as she scrambled to her feet, the indiscernible words of Monsieur Farel and Monsieur Roussel, the squeals of her mother's ladies. Jeanne felt her heart thud within her chest, as her mother pulled her up to stand.

Why is Papa so angry? she wondered.

He was shouting—saying terrible things to her mother—his eyes bulging, his hands flying wildly about. His face was so red that Jeanne wondered if it would burst, like a ripe tomato beneath the summer sun. Thoughts of tomatoes made her hungry. Her mother had brought her to her presence chamber after breakfast and that was a long time ago.

Jeanne didn't think it was very fair for her mother to expect her to endure the rigour of long prayers when she was only seven years old. But she had been taught to be obedient, so she had knelt quietly beside her mother, closed her eyes and tried not to think of ponies and apple orchards and the cook's good mince pies.

"And you have dragged our daughter into this heresy as well!"

Papa's shouted words snapped her attention away from prayers, pies and ponies. *Heresy?* She tested the word in her mind. *What did that mean?* She was about to ask, when her father strode forward, drew back his arm and struck her mother squarely across her face.

A strangled little cry escaped Jeanne, and she huddled closer to her mother, trying to bury herself in the folds of her voluminous silk gown. She tried to make herself small, praying that God would make Papa forget that she was standing right beneath him, but it was to no avail. He grabbed her by the shoulder and dragged her away from her mother's protective embrace.

"No!" she screamed, flailing against her father's bruising grip. "No! Mama! *Mama!*" Jeanne squealed and thrashed but her father simply picked her up, slung her over his shoulder like a sack of grain and strode out of the room.

"Wait! Henry!" she heard her mother cry.

Her father turned. "Your behaviour has consequences, Margaret," he snapped, sending goosebumps pebbling over Jeanne's arms. He then stalked away, Jeanne's slight form bouncing against his back.

Jeanne looked back at her mother, reaching out a pleading hand for her intervention. Her mother reached her own hand out towards Jeanne, tears slipping down her cheeks.

In that moment, Jeanne knew that Mama couldn't save her. She would have to face Papa's wrath alone.

Autumn, 1560

Memories swirled around Jeanne as she stood in her mother's old presence chamber—now her own.

"Am I intruding, Your Grace?"

Theodore Beza's voice broke into her reverie, and she pasted a smile on her face as she turned to face him. "Not at all, Monsieur Beza. Come in." She gestured for him to step into the room, then moved to the dais to seat herself beneath the canopy of state bearing the arms of Navarre. The memories would have to wait.

"You were deep in thought when I arrived," Beza said with a wan smile of his own.

"Deep in my memories," Jeanne murmured, her gaze assessing the kindly man before her. He perched upon the window ledge beside her, his face pensive. The quiet murmurs of her ladies created a soothing lull around them.

"Were they happy memories?" Beza asked suddenly, his penetrating gaze intent upon her face, assessing her as thoroughly as she assessed him. Jeanne glanced away.

"Did you know my parents, Monsieur?" she asked, smoothing her hand over her crimson silk skirt.

Beza's eyes flared in surprise at her abrupt question, but then he nodded. "I met your mother once, when I was very young."

Jeanne glanced at him in surprise. "Really? When? And where?"

Beza tipped his head, contemplating his answer. "I can't remember exactly when—sometime after 1528, I think. I was studying in Orléans under Master Melchior Wolmar and your mother summoned him to Bourges. I went with him."

Jeanne smiled. "My mother was one of the most refined, intelligent women in France," she said wistfully. "A tender, delicate soul with a backbone of steel." She paused. "Once, when I was a child, my mother brought me to this room. She had brought Monsieur Farel and Monsieur Roussel here, to preach to her and pray with her."

Beza's eyes widened. "William Farel and Gerard Roussel?" he clarified.

Jeanne nodded. "Two of the greatest French reformists."

"But your father—"

"My father hated reformists as much as he hated the Spanish," Jeanne confirmed. "Perhaps even more." She sighed. "He discovered us that day—all of us kneeling and praying in the reformist way, without the intervention of saints or popes or priests. He was so angry."

"What did he do?" Beza asked quietly.

"He slapped my mother across the face, then caned me." Jeanne shuddered. "I learned two things that day, Monsieur Beza," she said, looking him directly in the eye. "I learned that my father hated reformists, and I learned that my mother was brave enough to practise her faith regardless of what my father did to her."

"And you?" Beza asked, a gleam of challenge in his eyes.

Jeanne smiled. "I was too afraid to defy my father until he died," she admitted ruefully. "But as soon as he did, I embraced reform. My mother's example of courage and my cousin Renée's example of steadfastness convinced me that reform is not only necessary but just." She looked at Beza with determination. "My father wanted this realm to remain under the authority of the Roman Church. He persistently abused my mother to force her compliance, yet she never yielded to him. I am now queen of this kingdom, and I want to make sure her courage was not in vain."

A slow smile spread across Beza's face. "That is why you have invited me."

Jeanne nodded. "Not simply to minister to me—but to my people as well. I want Navarre to hear the good news of salvation, and I want . . ." she paused, raising a trembling hand to her lips.

"You want?" Beza prompted.

"I want to gain the courage to do what my mother never did," she whispered.

Beza nodded slowly. "You want to openly declare yourself in favour of the Reformation."

"Yes," Jeanne said, straightening her shoulders. "I want to openly embrace Protestantism."

"They will label you a Huguenot," Beza pointed out mildly.

Jeanne shrugged. "Then I will be the first Huguenot queen Christendom has ever had," she said.

Beza nodded approvingly. "Then we must ensure you are also the *best* queen it has ever had."

Pau, The Principality of Béarn, France
Winter, 1560–61

Jeanne felt like a woman balanced above a precipice. She knew the next step she took would plunge her into an abyss with no hope of return, yet she was strangely at peace.

It was Christmas Day. A day when everyone expected the Queen of Navarre, whose husband had just proclaimed his allegiance to the Roman Church, to be taking mass, like a good wife. But Jeanne had decided that she wanted to be a good disciple of Christ first.

"Are you certain you want to do this, Your Grace?" one of her ladies asked behind her. Her voice was filled with dread for she, too, knew the cost of what they were about to do.

Jeanne cast a sharp glance behind her, quelling the young woman's misgivings. "We are not cowards," she said resolutely. "We are soldiers going to war and we will not rest until we have obtained our freedom."

With that, she marched into the chapel and down the aisle, towards the waiting Huguenot minister who would change her life forever. He smiled uncertainly as though he, too, wondered about the wisdom of Jeanne's unprecedented actions. Jeanne returned his smile, took her place in the front pew, then nodded for him to begin.

The minister preached a rousing sermon, then administered communion in the Protestant fashion. After the service, she publicly proclaimed her change in allegiance, declaring to her subjects that she was embracing the Huguenot cause.

Chateau de Nerac, Navarre
Winter, 1561

When her husband, Antoine, burst into her privy chamber, Jeanne was prepared for his rage, though she had not imagined it would be so intense.

"What have you done?" he spat, stalking towards her, his eyes boring into her like blades.

Jeanne forced herself to remain immobile, holding his gaze unwaveringly. "I don't know what you mean—"

"You know precisely what I mean," Antoine snapped. "You attended a reformist service on Christmas Day of all days!"

Jeanne willed the nervous tension within her to dissipate. "You know that I have favoured reformist ideas for some time now," she pointed out.

He scoffed, dragging a hand through his hair and dislodging his cap, which fell heedlessly to the floor. Everyone around them in the chamber had frozen in petrified silence. "You waited until you were away from me—"

"You're the one who didn't want—"

"You went to Pau without me and publicly declared yourself a reformist heretic when you knew full well that I had declared myself a loyal son of the Holy Roman Church!"

Jeanne's mind raced back to that faraway day when her enraged father had burst into her mother's presence chamber, thundering and railing. Anger snapped her to her feet. "I am queen of this kingdom," she said coldly. "I am well within my rights to declare my religious affinity publicly."

Antoine stepped towards her, his hand balling into a fist beside him, twitching with energy waiting to be released.

"Don't you dare raise a hand to me," Jeanne said, hating herself for the tremor of fear that quivered through her voice.

Antoine narrowed his eyes and stepped back. He glared at her for several beats of heated silence before pivoting on his heel and stalking towards the entrance. "This isn't finished, Jeanne," he called over his shoulder. "You will live to regret this."

Jeanne stood trembling, staring at the space her husband had vacated. She reminded herself that she was Queen Regnant of Navarre, that Antoine was simply her consort, that his threats held no weight. Yet no matter how hard she tried to reassure herself of safety, dread turned her blood to ice.

Winter, 1563

Jeanne hurried along the narrow passageway of the palace, keeping pace with the silent guard who walked beside her. Urgency pervaded the air, wrapping her and the entourage who followed her in tense silence.

"Are the children ready?" she asked, when they reached the large double doors at the end of the passage.

"They are waiting in the carriage, Your Highness, as you instructed," the guard said stoically. He turned to the guards who stood watch behind her, nodding once, then with quick movements he opened the doors. The guards cocooned Jeanne and her maids, hustling them out into the icy air of the stable yard and up to the waiting carriage.

Jeanne was handed into the carriage ahead of the two maids. Before they were able to situate themselves, the guard shut the doors and the carriage lurched forward. Jeanne sank into the plush seat beside her son who immediately huddled close to her.

"Where are we going?" Henry whispered.

"We're going away for a while," Jeanne replied, wrapping an arm around his shaking frame and smoothing a soothing hand over his brow. She glanced at the nurse who held a bundled and sleeping Catherine in her arms. Her children were so young. Henry was only nine and Catherine barely four years old. They were too young to be thrust into such turmoil and Jeanne's heart clenched at the dangers ahead of them.

"Why must we leave Navarre?" Henry whined, burrowing deeper into her side.

"It's not safe here anymore," Jeanne said softly, stroking his head.

"Why isn't it safe?" he demanded.

"You must trust me, Henry," she said softly, running a finger down his cheek. "Mama is going to keep you both safe, but there is no time for questions now."

He slumped against her and said no more, too exhausted by their midnight departure to continue his interrogation. Jeanne stared ahead, watching the shadows play across the interior of the carriage and allowing her body to rock with its rhythmic sway. She didn't know how she was going to explain to Henry that they were leaving Navarre because his father had threatened to have her arrested and imprisoned.

Since an awful attack on a peaceful group of Huguenot worshippers in Vassy the year before, there had been war—Romanists fighting to kill and suppress Huguenots, Huguenots fighting to retain their freedom. Her husband had joined forces with the Romanists who fought against the Huguenots under the Duke of Guise. His participation in the war had only fuelled his anger against her for proclaiming the Principality of Béarn Protestant. Jeanne had been forced to increase her personal security and have a plan of escape wherever she went. Her proclamation had also garnered the ire of her cousin the King of France and his mother. Finding herself in increasing peril, she made the difficult decision to move herself and her children to Pau.

Despite the threats against her, Jeanne felt compelled to soldier on. Her mother had been Queen of Navarre. Her cousin Renée was Duchess of Ferrara. Yet, they were consorts, lacking the agency she now possessed as queen regnant—agency she was determined to use to further the gospel.

September, 1568

Jeanne's continued commitment to reform yielded increasingly dire consequences. Antoine had died of a bullet wound in Rouen, not long after her escape to Pau. Jeanne had returned to Navarre following his death, thinking that she and the children would be safe, but her hopes were soon dashed. The pope denounced her as a heretic, threatening to excommunicate her, confiscate her lands and grant permission to anyone seeking to invade her territories. And as if that weren't terrifying enough, she had recently received threats from Romanists in France and Spain. All of this had compelled her to run—again.

She turned away from her horse at the sound of approaching footsteps. Her children hurried towards her over the cobbled courtyard, their eyes wide and uncertain as they took in the scene before them.

"Are we going to war?" 14-year-old Henry asked, eyeing her large war-horse.

Jeanne forced a smile. "No," she said brightly, "we're going on an adventure."

Henry's expression turned doubtful.

"An adventure?" Catherine asked quietly. "With so many men and horses?"

Jeanne held back a sigh. Her children had grown up around conflict, which made them sensitive to the slightest shift in her mood and movements. She placed a hand on Henry's shoulder and drew Catherine close with her free arm.

"We must leave Navarre for a little while," she said.

Henry's jaw stiffened. "Is this like the last time we ran away?" he demanded.

Jeanne studied him in silence until his face contorted into a scowl.

"I am not a child, Mama," he announced. "If I am to be king one day, then you must treat me like a man."

Jeanne suppressed the urge to roll her eyes. Instead, she straightened, facing her belligerent son. "Threats have been made against your life and mine, Son," she said quietly.

Catherine gasped, clasping her hands tightly over her mouth. Henry paled but forced himself to remain rigid, unbending.

"Navarre is no longer safe. I believe La Rochelle is the safest place for us now, among other Huguenots."

"Is that why they have threatened us?" Catherine whispered. "Because we are Huguenots?"

Jeanne nodded with a sad smile. "They do not appreciate our convictions."

Silence stretched between them until Henry finally spoke. "Then we must go to La Rochelle," he said, resolution deepening across his face.

Releasing a relieved breath, Jeanne motioned for the grooms to help her children mount their horses, then turned to mount her own.

"Does Admiral Coligny know we are coming?" Henry asked, coming up beside her.

"I have sent word to him," Jeanne replied, raising her hand to signal her men to move forward.

She had recruited 50 gentlemen from her court to act as guards along the way, though heaven only knew if they would suffice. La Rochelle was a long way away and the French countryside was fraught with peril—especially for Huguenots. At times, as she had formulated her plan, Jeanne had wondered if leaving were as hazardous as remaining. In the end, she had decided to risk it.

They filed out of the quiet courtyard as dawn pearled the skies, hearts filled with anxiety and hope in equal measure. Jeanne prayed continuously for God's protection as they journeyed, fearing bands of looting brigands or companies of angry Romanist soldiers. Miraculously, God answered her prayers.

As they rode through the French countryside towards La Rochelle over the next 22 days, dozens of Huguenot soldiers crossed their path, choosing to journey with them. When they arrived at the gates of La Rochelle, Jeanne gazed around her in grateful amazement. God had sent an army to bring them to safety.

"Who goes there?" a watchman on the walls of La Rochelle called as they approached.

"It is I," Jeanne called back. "The Queen of Navarre." She smiled up at the watchman, throat tight, eyes gleaming with unshed tears. "I have come to seek refuge within your gates."

Jeanne d'Albret, Queen of Navarre, was born on November 16, 1528. Her father was Henry II, King of Navarre, and her mother was Margaret of Navarre, the Protestant sister of Francis I, King of France. Henry and Margaret's only child to survive infancy, Jeanne was heir to the throne of Navarre and the sovereign state of Béarn. Though Jeanne spent little time with her mother during her childhood, she was influenced by Margaret's faith. In a letter written to Nicolas de Flotard dated 1555, Jeanne describes the episode involving her parents that is mentioned at the beginning of this story.

It wasn't until her father's death in 1555 that Jeanne became more vocal about her Protestant faith. On Christmas Day, 1560, she publicly embraced Calvinism, and in 1561, she declared Béarn a Protestant state. When the French Wars of Religion broke out in 1562, Jeanne remained neutral, likely due to her relationship to the French monarchy. In 1563, she made concerted efforts to expand Protestantism in the French region of Guyenne. As a result, she was summoned before Pope Pius IV to answer to the charge of heresy. She was threatened with excommunication, the confiscation of her goods, an interdict upon her domain and permission to any who would and could invade her lands. Still, Jeanne did not yield. In September, 1568, fearing for her life and the life of her son, Jeanne took her children to La Rochelle where she sought refuge from the Catholic forces of France and Spain. She died only a few years later in 1572. Jeanne d'Albret was the first Protestant queen regnant.

13

Margarethe Prüss

THE LITTLE PRINT SHOP AT THE WOOD MARKET

The Free Imperial City of Strasbourg, Germany
Summer, 1524

Clement Ziegler attempted to stroll nonchalantly down Steinstrasse in Strasbourg, but the awareness of the sheaf of papers inside his jerkin made him as watchful as a hawk. It didn't help that he was easily recognisable. He was a gardener, but most people in the city knew him as a radical reformist who believed in strange ideas like adult baptism and the literal interpretation of Scripture. They called him and his kind Anabaptists. It was not a compliment.

When Clement reached his destination, he paused on the busy street, discreetly scanning his surroundings to ensure no-one was watching him. When he was satisfied that everyone was going about their business, he rapped quickly on the closed door. The establishment, which doubled as his brother's workshop and home, was closed for the day. He stood there waiting for what seemed like an eternity, impatience bubbling within him and the papers burning a hole in his clothing.

He rapped again—louder this time. Then he heard the tread of heavy footsteps, followed by the snick of the latch and the creak of the hinges as the door swung open.

"Well, it's about time," Jörg snapped, gesturing for Clement to enter.

Glaring at his brother, Clement shouldered past him into the dim confines of the shop. The long wooden table in the centre of the workroom was littered with scraps of cloth, ribbons, bobbins of thread and a jar of needles in various sizes. Shelves against the walls groaned beneath bolts of fabric. Clement marched through the room and down a short hallway to a large kitchen, which was crammed with a dozen red-faced, arguing men. Clement knew them all. They were artisans—most of them tailors like Jörg, but he also spied a few butchers, a strawcutter and a soapboiler. None of the city's gardeners were in attendance.

"I thought you were going to spread the word among your guild?" Jörg murmured in his ear as he slipped into the room behind him.

Clement shrugged noncommittally. He was still unsure of this group. They met regularly, but they couldn't seem to decide if they were pacifists or revolutionaries. The uncertainty chafed. Clement had seen what a mob could do.

As Clement surveyed the group, their agitation was palpable. At the front of the room, holding court before the fireplace, was Hans Adam, another tailor and one of Jörg's closest friends.

"What do you say, men?" Hans called.

"I say we storm the place today!" the strawcutter shouted.

A chorus of assent rippled around the room, followed by a spate of stamping feet. The scene was almost identical to a meeting Clement had led nearly a year ago, when the city council had first proposed the dissolution of monasteries in Strasbourg. Then, he had been among a crowd of gardeners who had decided to take it upon themselves to hasten that dissolution. He had since changed his views about the best course of action to bring about social and spiritual change.

"If we want to see reform, we must be courageous enough to grab it by the hands!" a butcher called.

The room was a keg of gunpowder waiting only for the right spark to ignite it.

"Tonight! We will go to Young St Peter's Church and tear down all their idols!" shouted a red-faced tailor, raising his fist in the air.

"We will reclaim Strasbourg for the gospel!"

"And lose your heads for your trouble," Clement heard his own voice cutting through the crowd.

Every man in the room swung towards him, taking him in as he leaned a shoulder against the wall, his arms folded across his chest. He tilted his chin to acknowledge their attention. "The gospel can no more be spread by violence and bloodshed than the Rhine can be lassoed at high tide."

"Jesus Himself upturned the tables in the temple and used a whip to chase out the moneylenders. How are we any different?" Hans challenged from the front of the room.

Clement pursed his lips. "And yet it was Jesus who commanded Peter to put away his sword and reminded him that those who live by the sword also die by its blade."

The heads of those present swivelled between the two men, unimpressed that their rousing meeting had been hijacked by a tardy gardener.

"So what do you propose we do?" Hans asked. "Sit idly by while the truth is trampled to the ground?"

"Do you honestly believe that you have no other recourse?" Clement replied. "Do you really think that the only way to effect change is to act like revolutionaries in the street?"

"No-one is going to shed blood," Jörg countered beside him. "We just want to help the town council implement the edict they issued to do away with monasteries and remove idols from churches."

"And your helpful intervention will only lead to riots," Clement reiterated. "The countryside has been burning since last summer because of peasant revolts. Strasbourg has been spared the violence thus far, but your actions will only inflame the situation."

"What do you propose we do, then?" Hans repeated, placing his hands on his hips and regarding him thoughtfully.

Clement strode to the front of the room and reached into the inner pocket of his jerkin.

"What's that?" a voice called.

Grinning triumphantly, Clement held the papers aloft. "This, my friends, is how we're going to bring change to Strasbourg!"

All her life, Margarethe Prüss had battled the predicament of being born a woman. Fortunately, she was not the type to let such challenges keep her from accomplishing her goals. Instead, she focused on the advantages she had been given—namely being the daughter of one of the most successful printers in Strasbourg.

When she was a child, Margarethe would sit on the floor of the little print shop at the wood market while her father worked, breathing in the scents of ink, parchment and vellum. She would peer at the large sheets leaving the press, ornately illuminated with stylised letters and beautiful woodcuts. When she was old enough, she began to work in the shop, assisting the various journeymen with their tasks until she had mastered every aspect of printing. She immersed herself in the process, drawing it into her veins through the osmosis of experience until words hummed in her blood. There was nothing she would rather do.

Margarethe's life had been a well-oiled machine until, suddenly and unexpectedly, her father died, throwing her into uncertainty. The uncertainty didn't last long though, because providentially and through a well-matched marriage, Prüss Press became hers. Well, hers through her husband. But it didn't matter. Margarethe was accustomed to living life through the proxy of a male relative. She couldn't own a business because business owners had to be citizens of Strasbourg and members of their trade guild of choice. Women could be neither. So she married a man who could be both. And when she was widowed, she remained undaunted. She simply married another printer, and now her life was humming along once more.

Margarethe was seated like a queen at her worktable, inspecting the accounts. Her husband Johann was at the press instructing a journeyman. Her children were underfoot. All was well with the world. Then the door to the press swung open to admit Clement Ziegler.

"I've come to see about printing a pamphlet," he announced, like a herald at the market cross proclaiming the dawn of the apocalypse.

Margarethe's head jerked up, Johann paused mid-sentence, and a hush fell over the pressroom.

"Herr Ziegler?" Johann asked uncertainly.

"I've come to see about printing a pamphlet," Ziegler repeated loudly, as though they had all gone deaf.

Margarethe regarded him with a small smile. Clement Ziegler was usually a troublemaker, but Margarethe had grown fond of troublemakers lately.

"Come into the back room," she said briskly, standing and stretching her back. "Ursula," she said, turning to the pale-faced young girl helping a journeyman set type.

"Yes, Mama?" Ursula dutifully answered.

"Look after the children." Margarethe nodded towards her numerous offspring, who were scattered about the pressroom.

Ursula nodded. "Yes, Mama."

Smiling, Margarethe motioned for the man to follow her, then led the way into the back room where Johann joined them. "What do you have for us, Herr Ziegler?" she asked, getting right down to business.

Clement pulled a small sheaf of papers from his jerkin and handed them to her. "I am hoping you might publish my pamphlet against the use of idols in church."

Margarethe considered the document critically. Ziegler wrote like he spoke—direct, rousing and a little rough around the edges. His style would appeal to many of the artisans in the city. The pamphlet was short but piercing, listing scriptural proof against the use of images. As she read, she handed each sheet to Johann to peruse.

As he came to the end of the document, Johann sighed and rubbed his forehead. "Strasbourg is more open to reform than other places, but printing this kind of thing is still risky."

Margarethe had known he would say that, and before Ziegler could utter a word, she jumped into the fray. "And yet we published Luther's works the year he appeared before the Emperor at Worms, which carried significantly more risk than this pamphlet does."

Johann gazed at her thoughtfully. The publication of Luther's work had been before his time, when Margarethe's first husband, Reinhard, had been alive. "You think this will sell?" he finally asked, deferring to her greater experience.

The fact that Johann Schwann was a printer had been one of the first things that had drawn a widowed Margarethe to him when she had considered remarriage. Unfortunately, he was not as experienced a printer as her first husband had been.

"I think it will be successful," she confirmed. "There are many in the city who are drawn to Anabaptist teachings—yourself included," she pointed out wryly. "It's hardly a stretch to think that there are others who would benefit from this work." Turning to Clement, she asked, "Why come to us? There are other printers in the city."

Clement raised an eyebrow. "Are you turning away my business?"

Margarethe remained impassive. She shrugged. "Merely trying to ascertain if this project is worth our time."

Clement swallowed. "I went to the city council for permission to publish but they denied me the right."

Johann groaned. "And you thought to come to us?"

"I thought to come to you because Prüss Press is known for printing material that is biblical. You published Luther's work when it was less than favourable to do so. You have published other reformists too, so I thought you might be inclined to take a chance on me."

Margarethe smiled. "I like taking a chance on people," she said. "And, more importantly, I like publishing work that will bring much-needed change." She turned to Johann and held out her hand for the manuscript. He obliged, keeping his eyes locked on hers.

"Are you sure?" he asked.

"Do you believe in what he has written?" she countered.

After a long pause, Johann nodded. "Yes, I do."

"Then you must publish it," she said simply.

Johann pursed his lips and rubbed his forehead. Finally, he exhaled and nodded. Turning to Clement, he extended his hand. "Herr Ziegler, you have found yourself a publisher."

Weeks later, Margarethe stood barefoot in the quiet pressroom, a taper burning low on the table beside her. She was clothed in a nightgown, her hair braided and tied off with a piece of cloth. The household was hushed in slumber, and she had taken the opportunity to creep downstairs to admire her latest creation. As she stood holding the small pamphlet by Clement Ziegler, she understood the gift she had been given. Words had the power to spread ideas, and ideas changed the world more effectively than war and bloodshed ever could.

With a happy sigh, she hugged the book to her chest, breathing a prayer of thanks that God had chosen her to do this work, in this place, at such a time as this.

Margarethe Prüss was born into a family that owned Prüss Press, a printing press in the Free Imperial City of Strasbourg. She was a daughter, sister, wife and mother-in-law of master printers and gained notoriety for being a printer in her own right, which was highly unusual for women during that period. After her father's death, Margarethe and her first husband, Reinhard Beck, took ownership of Prüss Press and published books that spread the Reformation, notably some of Martin Luther's work. During her subsequent marriages to Johann Schwann and Balthasar Beck, the press printed reformist writings that were radical for their time, including Anabaptist teachings. Margarethe also supported the work of other women, printing a hymnal edited by Katharina Zell and several volumes of work produced by Anabaptist women. At times, the books she printed were confiscated or burned, and on more than one occasion, she risked her life for her work. She died in 1542.

14

Renée of France

A Place of Greater Safety

Villa Consandolo, Argenta, Italy
Spring, 1536

Reneé despised being away from society—which was probably why her husband had chosen exile as a punishment. She had angered him by her continued defiance, and he had sent her packing to the edge of civilisation with a diminished court. She hated it, but not enough to yield to his wishes by recanting her faith.

"You knew it was coming," Michelle said, bustling up behind her as she stood gazing out at the thickly treed forest that surrounded the villa.

"Knowing and experiencing are two different things," Renée pointed out, lifting her arms as Michelle helped her dress.

"Well, moping about isn't going to do you any good. You must have a plan."

Renée nibbled on her lip, grunting softly as Michelle pulled and tucked her gown into place. "At least he allowed you to stay," she said, turning her head to catch Michelle's eye.

Michelle raised a brow, then stood back to scrutinise her handiwork. "He will ask me to leave shortly. I am certain of it."

Renée nodded. She was certain of this too. Her husband, Ercole d'Este, newly minted Duke of Ferrara, was a mercurial man—as short tempered as he was unpredictable. Everything had been just fine until his father had died the previous year, propelling him onto the ducal throne he now occupied. The sudden elevation had plunged him into uncertainty and insecurity. He knew what he wanted—the pope's favour, the emperor's favour, the French king's favour—but he could not fathom how to procure it all.

Renée had cast a pall over his ambitious plans by ardently embracing Luther's heresies. She had tried to be discreet, but Ercole had ferreted out her secrets. At first, he had been too preoccupied with matters of state to focus on her activities. But all that had changed after his official trip to Rome last autumn. He had set off determined to court the pope's favour and returned home dark and brooding. He had quickly become infuriated with her. He charged all her French courtiers with heresy and ordered them to return home.

The pinnacle of the crisis came when Ercole venomously told Renée that he wanted Michelle de Soubise, her childhood governess and her mother's closest friend, to return to France. Renée remembered the moment vividly. They had been seated on the terrace at their grand ducal residence, the Castello Estense, watching a masque after supper. It had all been so innocuous until her husband's words had crashed over her like a thunderclap. Renée had gaped at him in stunned silence for she could no more send Michelle back to France than cut off her own arm.

She had reasoned, pleaded and cajoled. She had written to her relatives in France—her cousin King Francis, his sister Margaret, every cardinal and bishop she could think of—pleading for their intervention. Their assistance had produced a small reprieve, but Renée knew her time was running out.

"And then that fool of a cantor had to go and make a spectacle of himself," she muttered, returning to the present.

Michelle turned her head sharply. "He was standing for what he believed!" she snapped. "Surely you don't begrudge him that?"

Renée sank onto the window seat and leaned her head against the cool glass. "No," she admitted wearily. "But I wonder if he had to do it so publicly."

Michelle rolled her eyes as she moved to sit beside her. "Renée," she admonished, "they were trying to force the man to kneel before the cross. He is a reformist. How could you expect him to betray his faith by kneeling to an object? It's idolatry." Michelle clucked her displeasure, watching Renée like a hawk. "Would you have done it?" she challenged when Renée remained obstinately silent.

Renée raised her head to look at Michelle. "Bowed to the cross?"

Michelle simply raised her brow.

Renée exhaled a resigned sigh as she shook her head. "No," she said softly, "I would not have bowed."

"Well, then, you can hardly expect him to have done so," Michelle pointed out.

Renée scoffed. "He could have refrained from kneeling without making a spectacle of himself."

The man, who had been tasked with leading the congregation in singing during the Easter service, had stormed out of the ducal chapel, scandalising the entire congregation. The local inquisitor had been present, and the display had prompted him to investigate not only the French cantor but every man and woman in Renée's court. Several of them had been detained for heresy. The debacle had ruptured Renée and Ercole's fragile marriage.

"He is so angry with me," Renée whispered.

"Who?" Michelle asked. "Your husband?"

"Yes," Renée replied. "That's why he's banished me here to Consandolo and taken the children away from me."

"Good grief, Renée!" Michelle exclaimed, exasperated. "I have never known you to sit around moping about your misfortunes. What are you going to do about that bully of a husband of yours?"

Renée glanced at Michelle, startled by her outburst. Her glowering face prompted Renée to grin. "You're right," she agreed. "I can't let him bully me. And neither I can I let him out-manoeuvre me in this game he's begun."

Michelle nodded, satisfaction gleaming in her eyes. "So what are you going to do?" she challenged.

Renée narrowed her eyes. "I'm going to beat him at his own game."

Summer, 1536

Summer brought a spate of terrible losses, leaving Renée feeling like a soldier returned from war.

Ercole had finally sent Michelle and her family back to France. Renée grieved her departure as keenly as she had grieved her own mother's death, yet Ercole remained implacable. He maintained that it was Michelle who had filled Renée's head with reformist nonsense. Renée could have told him that she had been fed a steady diet of reformist nonsense by Queen Margaret of Navarre since she was a child, but she didn't bother for she knew Ercole was deaf to her explanations.

Michelle had counselled her to relinquish the struggle. "Surrender this battle," she had insisted. "You have a war to fight, and this is the least of your concerns. Let him have this victory. It will make it easier for you to win others."

As usual, her old governess was as wise as she was indomitable. Renée had surrendered. Michelle and her children had been shipped off to France, leaving Ercole strutting about like a triumphant warlord. But Renée had not allowed his triumph to last long. She wrote to her cousin Francis, the King of France, lamenting Ercole's terrible behaviour towards her.

"He has deprived me of my three youngest children," she wrote. "What mother can bear such a plight?"

Francis had immediately come to her aid, persuading Ercole to reunite Renée with her children. Though Ercole had begrudgingly agreed, he exerted his control by insisting that she remain at the Villa Consandolo, away from the nucleus of the ducal court at the Castello Estense. He thought he was thwarting her but she had come to realise that he was inadvertently allowing her unimaginable freedom.

To avert Ercole's suspicions, Renée had offered up a feeble protest at his command before submitting to his wishes. She had since covertly embarked on turning her court into the biggest conclave of reformist thought Italy had ever seen. So far, away from Ercole's prying eyes, she was succeeding marvellously. Renée was presiding over her gloriously Protestant summer court when Clement Marot sidled up to her.

"Ah, Clement!" she exclaimed, smiling with delight. "Have you come to read me a poem?"

Clement bowed low. "No, Your Grace. Though I have been writing about you—a glorious epic, which I shall read to you when the time is right." At this, Renée beamed. "I am forever grateful that you offered me refuge here at your court when I was fleeing all that unpleasantness in France."

By unpleasantness, he meant nearly dying in the flames after the affair of the placards, a bungling attempt at denouncing the mass in Paris, which had led to the deaths of countless reformists at the hand of an enraged King Francis.

"I am not the only one who saved you," she pointed out magnanimously. "Her Grace, the Queen of Navarre sheltered you also."

"Indeed," Clement conceded, "but when things got rather . . . um . . . heated at the queen's court, I was fortunate that you agreed to shelter me here."

Renée nodded, graciously accepting his gratitude.

"I want to introduce you to someone," he began, and Renée's eyes brightened.

"Who?" she asked.

"A new intellectual, recently arrived from France." Clement turned to motion to someone behind him, but at that precise moment, the doors to Renée's presence chamber flew open and the Ferrarese guards outside pounded their halberds.

Dread pooled like ice in Renée's belly as she rose. There was only one reason the guards would behave so formally.

"His Grace, the Duke of Ferrara!" one of them shouted.

Renée wanted to bury her face in her hands. She was wholly unprepared for a visit, but powerless to now prevent one.

Her husband paused in the doorway, ahead of his entourage, then strode purposefully towards her, surveying the crowd of courtiers, who bowed to him obsequiously as he passed, their plumed hats veiling their faces. Ercole's gaze landed on Clement, whom he knew on sight. His eyes narrowed. Clement paled visibly but managed to bow.

Renée pasted a serene half smile on her face and curtsied deeply. "My lord husband," she said, "you honour me with your presence. Had I known you were coming, I would have made preparations for your arrival."

"I wanted to surprise you," Ercole replied, his reptilian eyes assessing her.

"And so you have," Renée breathed, meeting his gaze steadily. "You must be fatigued after your journey," she continued. "Why don't I—"

"No," Ercole said, sharply. He turned, motioning to a liveried groom to bring him a seat. "I would like to meet your court. I would like to see who graces your presence while I am away at the Castello." His glare penetrated Renée, as though he were trying to plumb the depths of her mind and uncover all her secrets. An inner tremor fissured through Renée, for she had many secrets to hide.

When a chair had been placed on the dais beside Renée, Ercole took his seat then turned to Clement Marot, who stood frozen like a statute before them. "Signor Marot," he said, flashing the man a false smile. "We meet again."

"Your Grace," Clement replied, gathering his wits enough to bow again. "I was just telling the duchess how I have been . . . er . . . busy composing some poetry."

"Yes, I know all about your poems," Ercole said, his smile dimming. "There are so many heretical thoughts intertwined within them, it's a wonder the King of France has not tossed you into the flames." Silence descended over the chamber like a pall.

"The King of France is gracious," Clement gulped.

"Or his sister is adept at interceding for heretics," Ercole observed acerbically.

"Have you met my friend?" Clement said suddenly, turning to the startled man beside him with a flourish. "This is Monsieur Charles d'Espeville—a visiting scholar from France."

Renée sucked in a sharp breath. This was the worst possible time to introduce an unknown and unexpected guest to her court. Who was this man? Was he a reformist?

"I was about to introduce him to the duchess when you arrived, Your Grace," Clement babbled, shoving d'Espeville forward.

The man bowed low, then looked up into Ercole's face, his dark eyes intense. Renée felt a jolt of recognition shudder through her. There was something familiar about this man. She studied his face, trying to place him. She was certain she had never met him before, but there was something about him that she recognised almost instinctively.

"Signor d'Espeville." Ercole greeted the man with icy disdain. "Why have you come to us?"

"I am a scholar, Your Grace," the man began, "drawn to your fine duchy by its intellectual culture."

At these words, Ercole began to soften; he fancied himself a renaissance ruler whose courts were filled with learned men from all corners of Christendom. Renée watched as Ercole conversed with d'Espeville on a range of topics and saw the tension drain from the room as her husband relaxed, smiled, and even seemed to enjoy the exchange.

Then the man said something—something that struck Renée deeply. She turned sharp eyes on him, scrutinising him until recognition dawned. Her gaze flicked to Clement, who was watching her closely, as though he had sensed the shift in her countenance. She widened her eyes at him, and he gave her an imperceptible nod. Renée settled back in her seat, struggling to arrange her face into an impassive mask.

God have mercy upon us! she prayed, her mind whirling. *What is John Calvin doing at my court?*

Renée liked to think of herself as a resourceful woman, but she found herself thoroughly discombobulated by the turn of events about her. First—Ercole arriving so suddenly, like a bird swooping down to eviscerate an unsuspecting mouse. Then—John Calvin appearing at her court, disguised as a French intellectual. Obviously, he had come seeking refuge—refuge she would have been only too happy to provide under normal circumstances—but with Ercole joining her court, the situation was volatile.

She was grateful that Calvin had managed to fool Ercole, though she was still uncertain how he had managed it. John Calvin was one of the most sought-after heretics in France. She knew that he had been forced to escape from the King of France just a few years ago. He had later returned to France, more determined to spread the gospel than ever, only to find himself evicted yet again in the aftermath of the placard affair. And now he was here. Without warning. At her court.

Renée alternated between elation and fear as she hurried down the long hallway of the villa, a maid in tow. She had told Monsieur Calvin to meet her in the orange gardens, which were on the opposite side of the villa from the rooms Ercole liked to occupy. She had to ascertain Calvin's plans. The darkness pressed in around Renée as she left the confines of the villa, picking her way towards the orange gardens with nothing but starlight to guide her way. She was wearing a hooded cloak and dressed in the plainest clothes she could find, but if discovered, they would both be in a terribly compromising position.

Finally, she saw Calvin standing beneath an orange tree, his figure limned in starlight, his own hooded cloak obscuring his face.

"Monsieur Calvin," she called softly, warning him of her approach. He turned towards her, and she felt his dark eyes watching her as she neared.

"You have taken a great risk to meet me like this, Your Grace."

"And you have taken a great risk coming here to Ferrara."

He hesitated. "Should I not have come?"

Renée shook her head. "No, I am glad you did. Did my cousin Margaret send you?"

"Not exactly," he replied. "I heard from others that your court is a haven for refugees such as myself."

"You heard correctly," Renée assured him, "though your timing has been unfortunate. I was not expecting my husband here at the villa."

A ghost of a smile curved his lips. "His Grace is a lively conversationalist."

"Thank the Lord you are too. You managed to convince him that you are nothing more than a French scholar."

Calvin shrugged. "I am a French scholar—though I am not only that."

Renée smiled. "Now, Monsieur Calvin," she said, "let us get down to business. How long do you propose to stay here? And what assistance can I offer you?"

After her rendezvous with Calvin was complete, Renée made her way back to her rooms, a small book clutched in her hands.

"A small gift—to thank you for your generosity in sheltering me," he had said.

It was a theological exposition of Christian faith and doctrine, written by Calvin, titled, *The Institutes of the Christian Religion*. He told Renée he had just completed it and urged her to read it. She promised she would.

When she reached her privy chamber, she laid aside her cloak, slipped into her nightgown and sat on the window seat gazing up into the sky. She knew the road before her was fraught with peril. Ercole had become her opponent. She knew he would be as wily as he was merciless. She knew he would brook no defiance, yet she could not relinquish her conscience to him. She knew what she believed, and she would not recant it simply because he tried to bully her into submission.

Bowing her head, Renée began to pray. She could not see the future, but she knew God could and she trusted Him to light her way one brave step at a time.

Renée of France, Duchess of Ferrara, was born to King Louis XII of France and Anne of Brittany on October 15, 1510. She is credited with saying, "If I had had a beard, I would have been the King of France." She married Ercole d'Este of Ferrara on May 28, 1528, at the age of 17, and they had five children. However, they later became estranged because of Renée's persistent reformist beliefs, and her husband deprived her of her home and children to pressure her to recant. Throughout her life, Renée was concerned for the safety of those persecuted for their faith. Despite the risks, she cultivated a court that became known as a place of refuge for Protestant reformers, such as John Calvin, who were fleeing persecution in other regions. The Roman Inquisition eventually put a stop to this. By 1550, conditions were so fearful that most Protestants had been forced to flee Ferrara. Ercole continued to pressure Renée to recant, using all manner of threats, until she eventually received mass in 1554. However, when Ercole died in 1559, Renée took up her Protestant faith once more. She chose to return to France and lived on her ancestral estates in Montagris, offering refuge to persecuted Huguenots during the French Wars of Religion. She died on June 12, 1575.

15

Anne Askew

THE FINAL WORD

The Guildhall, London, England
June 28, 1546

When Anne Askew was brought before the bishop's court for a formal hearing, she had lost count of all the prior hearings she had faced.

Truth be told, she was tired. All she wanted was to curl up on the window seat of her bedroom at South Kelsey Manor and have a nap. But she was far removed from the beloved house of her childhood and all its familiar comforts. She wanted to weep at the thought—to mourn over all she had lost—but she dared not shed a tear. Crying would make her look weak, and heaven knew they already considered her weak enough simply because she was a woman. Instead, she forced down her roiling emotions and eyed her fellow prisoners. She supposed they would be the subject of numerous alehouse jokes erelong: What do you get when you arraign a bishop, a merchant, a tailor and a gentlewoman?

Chaucer's Heretical Tales, she thought dryly.

She knew the proceedings would be swift and final for she had already submitted a written answer to their queries regarding her convictions. She did not believe that Christ was present in the host. She believed that to be the most appalling mummery ever invented.

She had even less use for confessing to a priest. All told, she was doomed to the flames.

Lord Chancellor Thomas Wriothesley rose from his seat to regard her with sly calculation. Anne felt a slither of icy dread snake down her spine. He began his interrogation without preamble.

"Do you stand by your opinion that the host is nothing but bread?"

Anne drew in a breath, steeling herself against what was to come. "I do, my lord."

"Do you deny that it is the very body and blood of Christ?"

"I do, my lord, for Christ is even now in heaven and will come again in the latter days in the same manner as he went up to heaven." She gazed directly into Wriothesley's eyes. "So you see, my lord, if Christ be in heaven, then he cannot be delivered to the earth by a priest mumming over a bit of bread."

There were gasps across the room, followed by the steady murmur of angry voices. Wriothesley's eyes never left hers. He gazed upon her like a falcon homing in on it prey, waiting only for the opportune moment to strike. Anne told herself that she was not afraid of him, but she couldn't convince her racing heart to agree to the dictates of her mind.

"And so you admit that you are a heretic," he said matter-of-factly, a glimmer of triumph flashing in his eyes.

"No, my lord, I am no heretic, nor do I deserve death, for I stand on nothing less than God's own Word."

Silence, thick and hostile, descended upon the room. The bishop, merchant and tailor all turned to gape at her. They had not been half so bold in their own answers. Anne cast them a sideways glance before returning her focus to Wriothesley. He nodded, seeming satisfied with her answer, then motioned for the guards to come forward.

"You have been found guilty of heresy, Mistress Kyme," he began.

"Askew," Anne countered loudly, loathing the use of her estranged husband's name coupled with hers. "My name is Anne Askew."

Wriothesley merely raised an eyebrow at her interruption. "You have been sentenced to death by burning at Smithfield Market upon a date and at such a time as this council will deem fit."

He motioned with his hand once more and the guards converged upon her. They led her out of the guildhall, down the steps and into a waiting wagon. She had expected to feel fear when she heard her sentence, or even dread, but she was suddenly overtaken by a desire to have the last word.

They had moved her from pillar to post, examining her for hour upon hour, forcing her to sign documents she was not given a chance to read and taking meticulous records of all that transpired. She had no control over what they said about her, no control over how they tried her or sentenced her or imprisoned her, but she was determined to regain control of her own story.

They might wish to inscribe her name in a book of heretical tales, but she was no heretic, and she would not allow them to make her one. Let them think they had silenced her by sentencing her to the flames. She would see to it that her voice came back to haunt them from the grave.

The Tower of London, England
June 29, 1546

Anne sat upon the small cot in a dank corner of the cell she occupied within the Tower. A shaft of light penetrated the room through the arrow loops in the wall above her, bathing her in its wan light and illuminating a writing desk and a rough table with an ewer and basin upon it.

"At least this place has less vermin than your cell at Newgate, mistress," said Mary. The company of a maid was one of the few privileges afforded an imprisoned gentlewoman.

"That's a mercy," Anne agreed. "But they haven't brought me to the Tower for my comfort. They must want something more from me than a recantation and public burning."

Mary looked at her in surprise. "What do you mean?" she whispered, hurrying to kneel before Anne. "What else could they want you for?"

Anne wearily rubbed her forehead. "I suspect they want more information regarding my association with the queen."

Mary gasped. "Do you suppose there is a plot against the queen?"

Anne shook her head, then shrugged. "I don't know. I have no inkling as to the machinations that surround the throne. What I do know is that when Richard Rich last questioned me, he looked like a cat preparing to devour a canary."

Anne grimaced as she thought about it. Sir Richard Rich was a powerful man—chancellor of the Court of Augmentations and a member of the king's privy council. He could do whatever he liked with her and no-one would raise a hand against him.

"Why take me out of prison—to the back room an alehouse of all places!—when they could have just questioned me at Newgate Prison, or even here at the Tower?" She shook her head, lapsing into silence as she contemplated her recent interrogation.

"That *is* strange," Mary agreed, breaking the silence.

Anne pursed her lips. "It must have been a ploy," she began slowly. "Plying me with good food and drink after nothing but prison rations." She drew in a breath. "I think they were hoping I might let my guard down long enough to give them the information they wanted."

"Information about the queen?" Mary confirmed, her agitation rising.

Anne nodded. "Sir Rich's questions were all so ambiguous. But he kept coming back to my association with the queen. He was friendly and menacing by turns. It was confusing—one moment he was feeding me, the next he was trying to bully information out of me."

"He's a cunning one, he is," Mary said bitterly.

Anne smiled wryly. "He would have to be to hold the kinds of positions he does. No-one could survive in King Henry's court if they weren't well versed in the art of subterfuge."

Mary sank back on her knees, watching Anne. "What do you think they'll do next?"

"They want information they believe I have," Anne began slowly. "They tried to coax it out of me in the alehouse, and when that failed, they brought me here." Her eyes widened as realisation dawned. "They're going to try to pry it out of me by force."

Mary's face paled. "But they would never . . ." She clamped a hand over her mouth to cut off the flow of words. "They don't use violence on gentlewomen," she finally whispered.

Anne rubbed her temple, which had begun to pound. "The Tower is only for the most hardened traitors. And if they believe I am guilty of treason, who knows what they will do to me?" A shudder rippled through her, pebbling her flesh with a chill.

They were silent for a moment, until Anne drew in a sharp, fortifying breath. "I cannot be certain why I was brought here, but I mean to make the most of whatever time I have left." She looked at Mary, her gaze full of urgency and meaning.

Mary nodded, acknowledging her unspoken request. "We must get on with our work."

Anne nodded. "Yes, we must finish it as quickly as we can, adding as much information as possible. You know what to do with it after . . ." Anne paused, swallowing hard. "After I am gone."

Mary bravely nodded, though her eyes were sheened with tears. "I know. I have all the information sewn into my cap and the coins sewn into the hem of my skirt." She patted the pristine white cap she wore over her curls for emphasis.

"Good," Anne said approvingly. "Now, fetch me the paper and the writing implements, and I shall get to it."

While Mary rummaged in her small sack for the necessary supplies, Anne lit the candle that stood upon the table from the fire burning low in the grate. She had used the meagre funds she had remaining, with Mary's aid, to write out a detailed description of all that had befallen her since she had been arrested. She was determined to make it as meticulous as possible. After her death, Mary was under strict instructions to take the missive out of England to John Bale, a reformer living in exile in Antwerp. Anne prayed that Master Bale would do his duty and publish her story in the Low Countries, ensuring that it could be smuggled into England in due time.

Anne began writing, feverishly scrawling down everything she remembered from her recent trials. It was well past noon when they heard footsteps outside their door. Mary immediately sprang to hide the writing implements and the half-finished manuscript while Anne composed herself.

The door groaned open, admitting Sir Richard Rich, followed by another councillor Anne did not recognize. Anne forced herself to remain still, not daring to glance at Mary, who had retreated to the farthest corner of the cell. Rich glanced at Mary, then turned his full attention to Anne.

"I want to know who else believes as you do," he said without preamble.

The hair on the back of Anne's neck stood to attention. So she had been right. He did want more from her. He wanted her to implicate other reformists. She remained silent, waiting for him to speak further.

Rich paced towards her and lowered his face to hers menacingly. "I want to know," he said, enunciating each word as though she were hard of hearing, "if the women in the queen's rooms believe as you do."

Anne heard Mary's soft gasp but forced her gaze to remain on Rich. Mary would crumble like a house of cards if Rich decided to interrogate her. Anne knew she must keep all his attention on herself.

"I know of no-one, my lord," she said.

Rich's jaw twitched. "Is the Duchess of Suffolk a heretic as you are?" he pressed. "What about Lady Hertford? Or Lady Denny? Or Lady Tyrwhit?"

Anne forced her face to remain immobile, but panic began to overwhelm her as she recognised the names. These were the queen's closest ladies—those of her inner circle who shared her reformist beliefs. If Anne implicated even one of them, who knew what the consequences would be? She shrugged, forcing a nonchalance she did not feel.

"I am somewhat acquainted with those ladies," she said calmly, carefully. "But I do not pretend to know the inner workings of their hearts."

Rich's eyes narrowed. "The king has been told that you are able to name a great number of heretics—especially those within the queen's rooms."

Anne tipped her head, regarding him with icy indifference.

"I regret to inform you that His Majesty has been misinformed," she said.

Sir Richard's face grew dark, and he opened his mouth to speak, but he was interrupted by Lord Chancellor Wriothesley, who strode into the cell as though he owned it, the Tower and all of England besides.

"Who gave you money when you were imprisoned in the Counter?" he demanded, bending over Anne.

She felt herself shrink but forced her spine to straighten. "No-one visited me in the Counter," she said firmly. "If I received any money at all, it was because Mary, my maid, went begging for charity from apprentices in the streets of London."

Wriothesley grinned in triumph. "And who, pray tell, were these mysterious and obliging apprentices?"

"I do not know," Anne replied with a shrug. When he turned his gaze upon a cowering Mary, Anne added, "I doubt Mary knows either. She is rather slow and dim-witted."

Wriothesley returned his serpentine gaze to her. "Do you know what I think, Mistress Kyme?" he asked, hooking his foot around the leg of the spare stool beside her and dragging it over. He sat down on it, towering over her as he leaned forward. "I think you're lying to me." He pushed back his bejewelled cap. "I think that some of your supporters, the most ardent and generous, perhaps, were not apprentices from Cheapside but gentlewomen of the court."

Anne remained stoic. "I suppose anything is possible, my lord," she said, flicking an imaginary piece of lint from her worn dress. "But even if it is as you say, you cannot hope to condemn them for their generosity."

"Stop prevaricating!" Wriothesley slammed his fist onto her desk. Anne jumped, her heart leaping into her throat. "I know for a fact that ladies from the queen's rooms sent you money. Who were they?"

"I only know what my maid told me," Anne blurted out without thinking. Once more she felt the eyes of all the men shift towards Mary, who released an audible whimper. "Once she was given 10 shillings by a man in a blue coat, who said the money came from Lady Hertford," Anne said quickly, desperate to draw their attention back to her. "Another time a servant in violet livery gave her eight shillings, saying Lady Denny sent it. That is what Mary told me." Anne sucked in a breath before adding, "There were apprentices as well. I did not lie when I said that. I have received money from a great many generous souls, but that is hardly an indication of their religious beliefs."

Anne pushed down the sting of tears as the men towered menacingly over her. They continued to question her for what seemed like hours. She maintained her position, refusing to implicate any of the ladies in the queen's rooms as heretics.

Finally, Wriothesley leapt from his stool with a frustrated growl. "Baker!" he snapped, motioning to the councillor who stood beside Rich. "Go fetch Kynvett."

Anne's fingers felt icy, and she darted a glance at Mary. *Oh dear God*, she prayed, *preserve me*.

It wasn't long before the Lieutenant of the Tower made his plodding appearance.

"Prepare the rack, Anthony," Wriothesley said without preamble.

Sir Anthony's eyes widened. "My lord?" he sputtered.

"You heard him," Rich snarled. "Do as he says and prepare the rack."

Sir Anthony hesitated.

"And who is to be racked, my lords?" he asked.

Wriothesley's gaze darted to Anne, and she felt all the blood drain from her head to pool at her toes. She swayed, gripping the table beside her to keep from toppling over into a heap on the floor.

"But she's a gentlewoman," Sir Anthony protested. "We know her father and brothers. I must protest in the strongest terms. We have never—"

Wriothesley grabbed Sir Anthony by his doublet and shoved him out of the room. "Prepare the rack, man, before I have you sent to the king for treason." Sir Anthony fled.

Wriothesley straightened his doublet and his cap, then turned to Anne and smiled—a startlingly charming smile. Bending, he offered her his arm. "Shall we, my dear?" he purred. "I believe you have a special appointment with the Duke of Exeter's daughter."

When Anne refused to take Lord Chancellor Wriothesley's arm, she was hauled off her stool by Master Rich, who manhandled her all the way from her cell, across the square and into the basement of the White Tower, where the instrument, derisively nicknamed after the man who had introduced it to England, stood.

When Anne came face to face with the implement of torture, she thought she would cast up her accounts. Never in all the history of the Tower had a gentlewoman been put upon the rack. She would be the first. She shivered, wishing with all her might that she would be spared the dubious honour.

"This is illegal," she began, summoning to mind some of the boring lessons that had been forced upon her as a child. "Magna Carta states . . ."

"Oh, be quiet!" Wriothesley snapped, jerking her towards the instrument of death and hauling her upon it with Rich's help. "I don't care what Magna Carta states. I have a royal mandate to find evidence against the queen and I intend to wring the truth out of you one way or another." Rich held her down as Wriothesley strapped her arms to the wooden frame. Then he divested himself of his cap and doublet and rolled up the sleeves of his expensive lace-trimmed shirt.

"Don't want my blood on your doublet, Lord Chancellor?" Anne heckled, unable to help herself. If they were going to rack her, then by all that was holy, she would not go down without a fight.

Wriothesley glowered at her with grim determination. "We shall see how blithe you are when we are done with you, Mistress Kyme."

When they were done with her, they dragged her back to her cell, where she fell onto the floor in a mangled heap. Her limbs were all dislocated, bent and sagging awkwardly about her body like sodden rags.

"Oh, mistress!" Mary cried as she bent over Anne, nervous hands fluttering about, uncertain where to land.

Anne groaned as she attempted to roll onto her back, but her arms wouldn't work. "Help me," she gasped, and Mary gently repositioned her. Anne cried out in agony, then lay panting, gazing up at the roof of her cell with tears of pain trailing down her temples and into her sweat-soaked hair.

Mary was silent, watching the agony that contorted Anne's face. "Did you—" she began, but Anne shook her head.

"They got nothing out of me," she said quietly.

Mary nodded. "Shall I fetch some—"

"Fetch my writing implements," Anne said, drawing in a shuddering breath.

Mary turned to her, aghast. "Your writing implements?"

Anne nodded. "Help me sit upright."

Mary hesitated, then acquiesced, wincing at Anne's muffled cries. When she was seated and resting against the wall, Anne jerked her head towards Mary once more. "Get the writing supplies," she panted between rasping breaths.

"But—"

"Do it!" Anne snapped through gritted teeth. She drew in a deep breath. "They think . . . they can bully me . . . into compliance," she said, forcing out each word through a haze of pain. "But they will not prevail." She pinned an insistent gaze upon Mary's face. "I want to record everything that happened in that room while it is fresh in my memory. Then I shall rest."

Smithfield loomed large in Anne's mind. She knew her death was near at hand. They would move swiftly now that she had given them nothing. But she had one last task to complete before they silenced her. She was determined to tell her story—to recount in faithful, brutal detail the atrocities she had suffered simply because she refused to recant her faith. She would tell her story not only so that justice might prevail but also to encourage others to hold fast to their faith regardless of the perils they faced.

Haltingly, Anne began to recount her experience, each word costing her far more than she was able to give, yet she persisted. Mary painstakingly recorded her words, weeping as she wrote. When Anne finished, she shut her eyes, spent.

"Remember the instructions I gave you," she muttered to Mary, her words slurred by pain and exhaustion.

"I won't fail you," Mary vowed, her voice hard. "Hundreds of years from now, when time and circumstance have erased us from the earth, your true account of all you have suffered shall endure, and it shall inspire others to follow your steadfast example."

Anne opened her eyes in surprise, overwhelmed by Mary's sublime words. Mary met her gaze with determination. "I shall see it done," she promised quietly.

Anne Askew was born in South Kelsey, Lincolnshire, around 1520 and likely received an early introduction to the Reformation and its beliefs through her brothers. She was forced by her father to marry Thomas Kyme, an ardent Catholic who abused Anne when he realised the strength of her Protestant beliefs. When Anne refused to recant, her husband violently expelled her from their home, denying her access to her children and possessions. Anne had no legal recourse and was denied a divorce.

The Final Word

Anne was a powerful speaker, and having committed large portions of Scripture to memory, she was also a strong biblical expositor. In London, her sister, who worked for Katherine Brandon, Duchess of Suffolk, introduced her to a growing circle of Protestant nobles. Anne preached to Queen Katherine Parr and her ladies-in-waiting on several occasions during the reign of King Henry VIII. She was eventually turned over to the authorities by a spy who accused her of Sacramentarianism—a refusal to accept transubstantiation. She was examined by the Bishop of London on several occasions, as well as by the Lord Chancellor of England, Thomas Wriothesley, and Richard Rich, a privy councillor. During these interrogations, she refused to recant or give up information that might incriminate others—even when she was tortured on the rack.

Her testimony, The Examinations of Anne Askew, *is one of the few documents written by a woman during the early modern period and provides an account that still promotes the causes of justice and faith today. Anne was burned at the stake at Smithfield on July 16, 1546.*

16

Elizabeth Tyrwhit

WORDS OF REVIVAL

London, England
Summer, 1546

Elizabeth Tyrwhit sat up with a gasp, trying to place the loud pounding that had woken her.

"My lady Tyrwhit," a woman's voice hissed. "Open the door!"

Eyes widening, Elizabeth whipped back the bedcovers and dashed to the door. Cracking it open, she peered out. The terrified face of one of the queen's ladies bobbed beside a glowing taper.

"What is it?" Elizabeth whispered.

"The queen has summoned you to her rooms at once."

"What?" Elizabeth gasped. "Why?"

The distressed gentlewoman cast a furtive glance along the darkened hallway before leaning in to whisper in Elizabeth's ear. "You are all in danger of being exposed before the king. The queen says you must hurry."

Elizabeth grabbed her robe, then hurried to follow the young woman down the twisting hallways to the queen's privy chamber. Inside, she found Queen Katherine Parr pacing and wringing her hands. Her sister Lady Anne, the Countess of Pembroke, was perched on a window seat watching her. They glanced up when Elizabeth entered.

"Eliza!" the queen cried, rushing to her side.

"What has happened, Your Grace?" Elizabeth asked, fumbling to curtsey.

"Dr Wendy has been to see me," the queen began, resuming her nervous pacing.

"The king's personal physician?" Elizabeth asked, her brow furrowing. She looked from the queen to her sister in surprise.

"He has uncovered a plot to arrest the queen and three of her closest ladies," Lady Anne explained, watching her sister's growing agitation with concern.

Elizabeth gaped at her. "A bill of attainder against the queen?" she whispered. Why had she heard nothing of this? "Who are the—" she began, but then stopped, realisation dawning with sickening swiftness. "I am one of the ladies?"

Lady Anne nodded, rising from her place at the oriole window to stand before Elizabeth. "The king suspects that the ladies of the queen's household are engaged in heretical practices," she said grimly.

"What do you expect will happen?" Elizabeth asked with equal gravity.

"The king plans to have you, Lady Maud Lane and I arrested and interrogated," Lady Anne said calmly.

"It is a ruse," the queen interjected. "Dr Wendy overheard a conversation between Stephen Gardiner and Tom Wriothesley."

The Bishop of Winchester and the Lord Chancellor of the Realm? Elizabeth willed her racing pulse to slow as she tried to make sense of this awful game.

"Once you are in custody," the queen continued, "they will have your rooms searched for forbidden books. If they find books contrary to the king's laws, they will have grounds to condemn you as heretics."

"And not us alone," Elizabeth breathed, appalled at the crude simplicity of the plan. "They will have grounds to find the queen guilty by association."

"And so be rid of her," Lady Anne finished, nodding.

The queen collapsed onto her bed, a sheen of perspiration on her forehead. "They want to be rid of me because of my reformist leanings," she said, twisting the long braid of her hair around her hand.

"And because of the influence you have over Prince Edward," Elizabeth said, slowly piecing the plot together in her mind. "They fear you are turning him into a true reformist." Gardiner and Wriothesley's loyalty to Rome meant they could not bear this.

"Edward is already a true reformist at heart," the queen whispered. "I believe he will be England's first truly reformist king."

And the Romanists at court would rather see us dead than allow such an eventuality, Elizabeth thought grimly. "What will we do?" she asked.

"I will go to the king and plead for clemency," said the queen. "I will plead for my life—for all our lives."

Elizabeth nodded, knotting her icy fingers together. She wondered if the queen's plan would work. King Henry was notoriously mercurial. He was as likely to chop off all their heads as he was to grant them mercy.

"I want you to go to your room, Eliza," the queen said, interrupting Elizabeth's wild imaginings. "I want you to dispose of every incriminating book you can find. I will do the same. We have summoned Lord Parr, my uncle, to retrieve my books. I suggest you send for your husband to retrieve yours."

Nodding, Elizabeth rose to take her leave. But as she reached the door, the queen called her name. Looking back over her shoulder, Elizabeth took in Katherine Parr's bloodless face.

"Pray, Eliza," she urged softly. "I fear we may all lose our lives by week's end."

Elizabeth hunted down every reformist book she kept with her at court. She unearthed dozens dealing with topics that could see her burned as a heretic—the primacy of Scripture, justification by faith, the priesthood of all believers, the commemorative nature of communion—and every book by Luther she possessed.

As she added to the growing stack, her hands trembled with trepidation. Her books were the lifeblood of her Christian experience, nourishing her, encouraging her, helping her gain clearer perspectives of Scripture. It pained her to part with them. *Better to send them to the country than see them burned*, she told herself. *Or be burned because of them*. Elizabeth shuddered.

She was in the process of hurriedly searching beneath her mattress when her husband charged in, hair dishevelled and eyes wild as he surveyed the piles of books on the floor.

"Good heavens, Eliza!" he whispered urgently. "What are you doing? What has happened?"

Elizabeth grunted as she hefted her mattress higher to reach a book wedged deep beneath. "I need to get rid of these books, Rob."

Robert rushed to help her, but when he saw that the book she had extracted was one of Luther's, his eyes widened.

"Why do you have all this contraband in your room at the palace?" he breathed. "Right under the king's nose!"

Elizabeth gathered an armful of books from the floor and hurried to put them in a small trunk open by the hearth. "Did you not know I brought them from home?" she asked, carefully laying them inside.

Robert glanced between his wife and the books, rubbing his forehead in bewilderment. "I had no idea," he replied. He quickly picked up a stack of books and handed them to her. "Are you in danger?"

Elizabeth told him about the plot as briefly as possible, watching his jaw slacken with each word.

"Oh, don't look so shocked," she snapped irritably, shutting the lid of the trunk, then leaning on it to fasten the clasp. "You knew what we were doing in the queen's rooms. Besides, you believe all of it yourself."

Robert groaned. "For the love of heaven, Eliza! I knew of some of your activities, but I didn't realise that you had caught the attention of Bishop Gardiner and the Lord Chancellor. Do you know what they did to Mistress Askew?"

Elizabeth paused, slumping against the trunk of books. "I know," she said quietly. The Lord Chancellor had personally racked her in the Tower of London, trying to squeeze a recantation out of her.

Robert crouched beside her. "Did you not think the same could happen to you?" he asked softly.

She bit her lip, then shook her head. "I thought we would be safe so close to the throne."

Robert shook his head, dragging a hand over his face. "Have you not read Master Wyatt's poem?" he asked, eyeing her in disbelief.

Of course she had. They all had. "*Circa Regna tonat*," she recited, rising to her feet.

"Thunder rolls around the throne," Robert repeated, standing with her. "And being so close to the storm, you are bound to be struck by it."

"Not if you help me smuggle these books out," she countered.

For a moment, Robert looked tempted to continue chastising his errant wife, but then he expelled a breath. There was no time to lose. Bending to heft one end of the trunk, he motioned for Elizabeth to pick up the other.

"Come on, then," he said. "If you don't want to get caught, you're going to have to carry your share of the load."

The Manor of Leighton Bromswold, Huntingdonshire Summer, 1553

Elizabeth watched the rider as he approached the manor, a small puff of dust in the distance the only visible indication of his advance. She turned from the window and went in search of Robert, finding him in the stables already astride a horse.

"A rider is approaching," she said breathlessly, laying a hand on the bridle.

Robert frowned, then swung out of the saddle, tossing the reins to a groom. "It must be news of the king," he said finally.

Elizabeth nodded. "It has to be," she agreed.

They paused in the stable yard, looking at one another silently.

"Mary will take the throne," Robert finally said. "Regardless of the king's plans."

Elizabeth nodded again, a frown crinkling her brow. "How will we survive?" she asked.

Robert smiled wryly. "The same way we survived the incident with Queen Katherine and the forbidden books," he said. "We must think and act quickly."

He led the way back into the house, tugging off his gloves. Elizabeth trailed after him, lost in thought. The debacle with the banned books had taught her vigilance, especially around the throne. Somehow, they had managed to escape that disaster unscathed.

King Henry had died not a year later, allowing them to enjoy six peaceful years under the reign of his reformist son, King Edward. Then Edward had been struck down by a wasting illness that whittled away his young life. The last they had heard, he was near death and planning to bequeath the throne to his cousin Lady Jane Grey, whom he believed to be England's only hope of remaining reformist. His decision to bypass his sisters in the succession was not a popular one. Elizabeth knew enough about court politics to know that heads would roll in the aftermath of the king's death.

When they reached Robert's office, he shut the door and faced her. "We need a plan."

Elizabeth agreed. They were staunch reformists. Mary Tudor, the legitimate and most likely candidate for queen was a Romanist. "She will get rid of all the leading reformists," she said, pacing. "Cranmer, Latimer, Nicholas Ridley . . ."

Robert nodded, watching her. "Anyone who has been outspoken in their views."

Elizabeth paused to face him. "Which includes us—mostly me."

Robert rubbed his forehead.

"I know Princess Mary," Elizabeth said slowly. "When I attended Queen Katherine, she was close to the queen. She frequented the queen's rooms. She was always there when we were reading Scripture in the afternoons. She even helped us translate Erasmus's paraphrases into English."

Robert raised a brow. "Indeed?"

Elizabeth nodded, excitement building within her. "Yes, she translated nearly the entire gospel of John."

"That does not mean she is in favour of reform," Robert noted. "Her views are well known."

"No," Elizabeth agreed, "she most definitely is not, but our association may make her willing to overlook us—favour us even—if we play our cards right."

"What do you propose to do?" Robert asked.

Elizabeth tapped her lips. "We need to lie low and show her our loyalty without compromising our faith. If we steer clear of her court, I think we might be able to pull it off."

Robert considered this. "Do you think that will suffice?"

Elizabeth shrugged. "*Circa Regna tonat,* remember? If we stay as far away from the throne as we possibly can, perhaps we shall be spared its rumblings."

Robert nodded slowly. "It's worth a try," he agreed cautiously. Then suddenly he frowned. "Will you pretend to be a Romanist?"

"Will you?" she asked.

He shook his head. "I couldn't. It would be a betrayal of everything I believe."

"Exactly," Elizabeth nodded. "No, I will continue to nurture my faith. Better yet, I am determined to help other women nurture theirs."

"Eliza," Robert warned, but she cut him off with a dismissive wave.

"Don't worry," she said. "I shall not be caught."

"You shall not be caught?" he asked incredulously. "For heaven's sake, Eliza! Mary will be twice as exacting as King Henry was in matters of religion. How do you plan to evade her?"

Elizabeth shot him a sly smile. "I have a plan. One that involves paper and ink."

A groom knocked on the door and announced the arrival of the messenger. Robert groaned. "Whenever you are involved with paper and ink, there's always trouble," he muttered, striding towards the door and flinging it open.

Spring, 1554

"You are going to get us both killed," Robert said, staring down at the small manuscript in his hands.

"No, I'm not," Elizabeth said. "At least I don't think so." She furrowed her brow at him. "You're not planning on getting caught, are you?"

He raised his head to glare at her. "I don't plan on it, but that doesn't mean it won't happen," he snapped. He turned the book over in his hands. "This is what you have been working on?" he asked more gently.

Elizabeth nodded, clasping her hands before her. "It is a prayer book," she said, "setting out the tenants of the reformist faith in the form of prayers." She had worked on her project night and day, praying fervently for God's guidance. She knew that though her reach was small, God's was not. She knew that her effectiveness in nurturing reform lay not in her might or in her power but in the potency of God's Spirit.

Robert opened the book, turning the stiff leaves with care.

"The primacy of Scripture, justification by faith, the priesthood of all believers, the commemorative nature of communion—all of it is there." Elizabeth chewed her lip nervously as she watched him.

"If Queen Mary catches wind of this, she'll send you to the Tower right along with her sister," Robert muttered, tracing his finger along a hand-written page.

"I know, but it will be worth it. Imagine, Rob. If I can make copies of this book, I can distribute it in secret to other women. It could help to keep the faith alive in England, even as Queen Mary is working with determination to snuff it out."

"So, this was your plan," he murmured, glancing up at her. "A book."

She nodded. "Words have power. They can touch hearts, transform minds. Think of the influence the reformers have wielded simply by putting quill to paper. Tyndale, Luther, Calvin, Knox—they have filled all of Christendom with the truth." Elizabeth pursed her lips in determination. "I mean to do my part—small though it may be—to keep the Reformation alive in England. " She nodded towards the book he held. "And this is how I shall do it."

Robert shut the book and tucked it into the pocket of his doublet. "Will you have it printed?" he asked, gazing at her with a mixture of fondness and anxiety.

Elizabeth shook her head. "Not just yet. Perhaps in time. Mary still means to marry and produce an heir if she can. Who knows what will become of us all if that happens? Perhaps the only way I will ever distribute this is by transcribing it myself—but I suppose we shall see."

Robert nodded.

"So will you do it?" she asked.

Her husband smiled at her, shaking his head. "You are a troublemaker, Eliza Tyrwhit, and God help me for I have become your willing accomplice. I will try to do as you ask, though it may be harder to smuggle this into the Tower than you believe." He shot her a warning look. "And even harder to ensure it reaches Princess Elizabeth."

"But you will try," Elizabeth insisted, "for she is sorely in need of encouragement, imprisoned as she is inside that ghastly place."

Robert's smile softened. "Yes, she does need encouragement," he agreed. "I will do my best to make sure she gets it." He patted his pocket to lend credence to his vow.

Later, as Elizabeth watched her husband ride away from the manor, she said a small prayer for him and for the recipient of the book. She might not be a preacher or even a teacher, but she was determined to use what resources she had to keep the light of truth alive in England—no matter the cost.

Elizabeth Tyrwhit (née Oxenbridge) was born sometime before 1510. Her parents, Sir Goddard and Lady Anne Oxenbridge, were minor members of the English aristocracy, and Elizabeth served as a lady-in-waiting to both Queen Jane Seymour and Queen Katherine Parr during the reign of King Henry VIII. She and her courtier husband, Sir Robert Tyrwhit, had one daughter, Katherine. Elizabeth fervently embraced the Reformation alongside Queen Katherine and was so well versed in Scripture that her husband once jokingly remarked that she was "half a Scripture woman."

When Mary I ascended the throne, Elizabeth withdrew to her estate in Huntingdonshire and began working on her book Morning and Evening Prayers. *She was the first woman of the Reformation to write a prayer book, which not only incorporated her own spiritual beliefs but also the basic theological framework of Protestantism. Historical sources strongly indicate that she smuggled a copy of this book to Princess Elizabeth when she was confined in the Tower of London during her sister's reign. When Elizabeth I became Queen of England, Elizabeth Tyrwhit's book was among the Protestant literature that was printed and freely distributed throughout England.*

17

Elizabeth Welsh

THE SCHOOL OF HARD KNOCKS

Leith Pier, Edinburgh, Scotland
November 7, 1606

Elizabeth navigated the long pier, a slender figure framed by a dawn-bright sky ribboned with rose and grey. The wind bit into her, hissing through the thin layers of her clothes to sink its teeth into her bones. Above her towered the silhouettes of countless ships, their dark shapes bobbing in the waters of the harbour. The wharf bustled with life. She wove around stevedores lading goods, sailors hefting great coils of salt-encrusted rope and merchants keeping a wary eye on their seagoing cargo. Everyone jostled for purchase on the rough-hewn walkway strewn with casks, crates and sundry goods. Elizabeth kept her eyes fixed on a single vessel at the far side of the harbour and the small group of men beneath its shadow who were waiting to board.

"You're here!" her husband John exclaimed softly, gathering her into a tight embrace before setting her away to scrutinise her face. "When did you arrive?"

"Last night," Elizabeth responded breathlessly. "I went home after your trial as we agreed, but I couldn't bear to have you leave Scotland without seeing you again. I came on horseback."

His eyes sharpened at this bit of news. "Alone?"

Elizabeth shook her head, nestling against him to shelter from the wind. "No, I brought one of the servants. And before you ask, the children are well. They miss you and send their love, but we are all relived that you are being exiled, not hanged."

John laughed low as he drew her close once more. "Yes, God be praised for that."

One of the other men cleared his throat loudly before announcing that they would conduct a small service of thanksgiving and supplication before they set off on their voyage. Elizabeth fitted her hand into the crook of her husband's elbow and leaned against him. He was a skeletal shadow of himself, but she was too immensely grateful that he was alive to care. He had come too close to swinging from the end of a rope at the market cross for her peace of mind.

As the minister began the service, Elizabeth's exhausted mind wandered. She was no stranger to spiritual warfare—she had been raised on a steady diet of reformist tales since she was a child. The stories she loved best were the ones involving her father, the indomitable John Knox. Elizabeth understood the courage required to stand for one's faith—the sacrifice and commitment of those facing persecution, and their families, as well. Yet she had grown up in a peaceful Scotland. A place where reform was accepted and embraced. She had never seen anyone burned or hanged. Perhaps that was why she hadn't thought twice about marrying a minister. How the tide had turned in a few short months! She shivered and John drew her closer to his side.

"Are you cold?" he whispered in her ear.

Elizabeth shook her head. No, she was not cold, just suspended between relief and dread at what lay before them.

When the service ended, the men turned to farewell loved ones who had gathered on the pier. John gave Elizabeth a hard hug.

"I'll see you in a few months," he said, gazing down at her. "When I'm settled, I'll send for you and the children."

She nodded, too overcome with emotion to speak. How had it come to this? One day the Scots Kirk had been free and the next hostage to the whims of a volatile monarch.

"Do you think the French will treat us better than our own king?" she whispered.

"Probably not," John said with a wry smile. "But I would rather live in France than be buried in Scotland, don't you agree?"

Elizabeth sighed. "Why could he not simply have left us alone?" she wondered out loud, not for the first time.

"The king has his reasons," John said quietly, "the chief of which is to enlarge his power."

Elizabeth knew this was true, but it still rankled. "Can't he simply be content with ruling two kingdoms?" she demanded. "For years, the Scots have fought the English. And now look at us—a Scots king on the English throne. King James should content himself with that conquest instead of trying to unite the Scots Kirk with the Church of England. Can't he see that it's a fool's errand?"

"*Shhh*," John hissed, glancing around nervously. "Don't go calling the king a fool in the middle of Edinburgh," he warned her. "Besides, talking about the king's wishes isn't going to change them. He wants to rule over the Scots Kirk just as the kings of England rule over the English Church. He's not going to take no for an answer."

Elizabeth gazed up at him, admiration shining in her eyes. "I'm proud of you," she said softly.

A year ago, her husband and several other ministers of the Scots Kirk had refused to submit to the king's demands. They had maintained that the Church of Scotland should remain free from the influence of the king. Christ was the head of the church, and no earthly ruler had the right to usurp that authority. They had been arrested, imprisoned and tried for their forthrightness. A jury had found them guilty of treason, a sentence that carried the death penalty, but the king, for some inexplicable reason, had intervened, exiling them to France instead. Elizabeth was grateful for that small mercy, but her spirit chafed against the oppressive rule of a monarch who sought to curtail the freedom of her conscience.

"If my father were alive . . ." she muttered.

John laughed. "If your father were alive, King James would have been hard pressed to know what to do with him."

Elizabeth giggled, then sobered. "Send for us when you are settled, John Welsh," she said, pressing herself against her husband.

"I will," John promised. After a final embrace, he followed the other ministers up the gangway onto the ship.

Elizabeth stood on the pier long after their ship had passed from view, contemplating what the future might hold.

Jonsack, Angoumois, France
Summer, 1607

France turned out to be a nightmare. Before she arrived, Elizabeth had imagined that ministering to free Huguenot congregations would surely be an improvement on their situation—but she soon learned that she was wrong.

"Why do they hate us so?" she cried to John one night after the children had all been put to bed. Her head throbbed with each beat of her heart, and her eyes stung painfully. She had been almost continuously ill since arriving in France, as had the children.

"I don't know if they hate us," John muttered, sinking onto their narrow bed with a weary sigh.

"Then why do they treat us so poorly?" Elizabeth demanded, tears gathering in her eyes and tightening her throat. "They refuse to pay you. We live in a hovel, and the poor nutrition and appalling living conditions are making us too sick to be of any use to anyone." Sinking down beside him, she buried her face in her hands, battling the urge to wail.

John wrapped his arm around her shoulders. "I have spoken to the consistory, and they have agreed to take action against our congregation."

Elizabeth raised her head. "Will that do any good? Or will it only make them more bitter towards us? Heaven knows, we don't need to stoke the flames of their ire any further."

John rubbed his forehead. "I don't know what else we can do," he said helplessly. "I never dreamed we would be treated so poorly." He glanced at her. "Did you manage to get some provisions from the market today?"

Elizabeth nodded. "Yes, but barely enough to feed us for a week. I'm being careful with the funds I brought from home, but if the congregation doesn't pay us soon, we will starve." She drew in a shuddering breath. "I'm most concerned about the children, John. I don't think I could bear it if one of them . . ." She paused, pressing a trembling hand to her eyes. "Children are so vulnerable," she whispered, unable to finish her thought.

John was silent. He, too, knew that if they didn't get adequate nourishment and proper lodgings soon someone would die.

Unable to bear it, Elizabeth buried her face in her hands and wept. *Oh, God!* she cried out in prayer, as anguish gripped her soul. *Please have mercy on us!*

London, England
Spring, 1622

After repeated pleas for clemency and relief, the king had finally granted them permission to return from exile. But only as far as London. Elizabeth gazed out at the fog-obscured streets, vacillating between grief and hope. John's health was almost irretrievably broken, as was hers. When the king had finally granted them permission to enter England, they had both been on the brink of death. All Elizabeth wanted was to return home—to Scotland—but permission to do so remained in the king's gift, and he was a cruel, tightfisted man.

The door opened, admitting a sombre-faced John, who took her measure with a critical eye. "Are you certain you are able to do this?" he asked, when she simply stared at him wordlessly.

The School of Hard Knocks

Elizabeth returned her gaze to the window. "What choice do we have?" she asked, bitterness creeping into her voice. "If I want to return home and save my husband's life, I must go and grovel before the man who caused my daughter to die."

It had been seven years since she had watched the face of her firstborn slacken in death, emaciated by malnourishment and illness, yet the sting was still fresh. Elizabeth felt John's arms encircle her shaking shoulders. He said nothing. There was nothing that could dispel the anguish in her soul. He simply stood there holding her as she willed back the deluge of tears. After a moment, he gently set her away from him and gazed into her face.

"God will be your strength and your refuge," he said softly. "He has not abandoned us, Eliza, not even in our darkest hour. We must still cling to the truth of His goodness and forge ahead. Remember who you are." He squeezed her shoulders as though bracing her for battle. "And more importantly, remember who you represent."

The king had granted Elizabeth an audience. Her mother was a Stewart, which made her one of the monarch's distant cousins, but Elizabeth did not expect this familial tie to merit much of his favour. Dressed in a borrowed gown, she boarded a wherry to Greenwich Palace. As she journeyed up the Thames, she recalled a story she had heard as a child about how her father had stood before the king's mother at Holyrood Palace in Edinburgh. The young Mary, Queen of Scots, had been reduced to tears during that encounter. Elizabeth doubted that she would reduce the king to tears, and she fervently prayed that he wouldn't bring her to that juncture either. Nevertheless, the story shored up her courage.

When she was ushered into the king's presence chamber, his courtiers glanced at her curiously. Steeling her resolve, Elizabeth raised her chin and marched forward, dropping into a deep curtsey before rising to stand before the king. She kept her head meekly bowed, lashes lowered, but her mind was blazing with a thousand arguments.

"Well, what is it?" the king demanded, with an impatient flick of his wrist.

"Your Majesty," Elizabeth began softly.

"Speak up, madam," he snapped. "I don't have all day."

Elizabeth bristled, forgot herself for a moment and raised her chin to stare directly at the king, eyes sparking with fury. She presented her case before him quickly, holding on to her temper by the barest of threads. Her husband John Welsh had been exiled to France for treason. Did the king remember him?

An appalled murmur rippled around the room, but Elizabeth continued undaunted, explaining their miserable living conditions, the ill treatment they had suffered at the hands of the French, their continuously ill health and the death of their beloved daughter. When Elizabeth recounted this detail, her voice broke and she was forced to lower her face.

"Please," she said to the king, holding on to as much dignity as she could as she begged, "please allow us to return home to Scotland. My husband's health is dismal. I fear he may die without intervention of some sort."

The king studied Elizabeth for what seemed like an eternity before he asked, "Who was your father?"

"John Knox," she replied calmly.

His eyes widened and an oath burst from his lips. More murmurs rippled across the room. "Knox and Welsh!" he exclaimed. "The devil never made such a match as that!"

"Most likely he didn't, sir," Elizabeth retorted. "For we certainly didn't solicit his advice."

The king grunted. "And you say you lost a daughter? How many children do you have?"

"Three," Elizabeth replied.

"And are they lads or lasses?"

"All lasses."

"God be thanked!" he cried. "For if you had three lads, none of my three kingdoms would have had a moment's peace."

Elizabeth chose to ignore that comment and returned to the matter at hand. "Please, sir. My husband needs to go home. Please allow him to have his native air."

"Give him his native air!" the king exclaimed, rising agitatedly. "I'd rather give him to the devil!"

"You can feed your courtiers to the devil, sir, and instead spare my husband's life for he has been nothing but a loyal subject," Elizabeth snapped, forgetting that she was speaking to the King of Great Britain.

The king was silent for a moment, fuming as he glared at her until his expression shifted into grim resolution. "If he will submit to my requirements," he said, pointing a bony finger in Elizabeth's face, "I will allow him to return home."

Elizabeth's mouth tightened and she made the king a shallow curtsey. The king regarded her with a triumphant gleam in his eye. He lifted his chin, opening his mouth to speak but Elizabeth raised her hand before he could utter a word. "I would rather see my husband hanged," she told the king icily, "than watch him violate his conscience." Then, without waiting for further reply, Elizabeth withdrew from the room with as much dignity as if she were Queen of Scotland and he her wayward subject.

When she returned to their lodgings in London and recounted her tale, John gaped in shock.

"You didn't speak to the king like that," he breathed.

"King or not, I was not about to let him walk all over me," she ground out.

John smiled at his wife's determination.

"Put not your trust in princes, nor in the son of man in whom there is no help," she quoted, taking his hand. "God is our refuge, John. He is our help. Should I have told the king that you were willing to submit to his demands in violation of your conscience?"

John squeezed her hand. "No, you did right."

Elizabeth nodded. "Then God will see us through this, and we will remain faithful to Him whatever the cost."

John nodded, then grinned. "I wish I'd been there to see it."

Elizabeth blushed and swatted his arm. "You speak as though I were some performer on a stage."

"Even better," he said, drawing her in as his grin widened, "you're Knox's daughter, sparring with another Stewart monarch. I bet we could have found a crowd of people who would have paid good money to see that."

Elizabeth Welsh (neé Knox) was born around 1568 to John Knox and his second wife, Margaret Stewart. The exact date of her marriage to minister John Welsh is unknown, but they were definitely married by the summer of 1596. When James VI acceded to the throne of England, he sought to appoint himself head of the Church of Scotland. John Welsh and others were arrested for protesting against the king and found guilty of treason, a crime punishable by death. However, the king instead exiled them from Scotland, forbidding them to return on pain of death. Elizabeth is remembered for her passionate advocacy before the king on behalf of her husband. The exchange was tense and combative, especially when the king discovered who Elizabeth's father was. Some of the dialogue in this story is based on historical reports of the exchange between Elizabeth and the king. The Welshes were forced to remain in London and John Welsh died there around May, 1622. Elizabeth died soon after in January, 1625.

18

Marie Durand, Isabeau Menet and Anne Goutez

A Bond That Strengthens

Pont-Saint-Esprit, France
March, 1737

Someone was screaming—awful blood curdling wails that bounced off the prison walls. Isabeau Menet numbly wondered who was in such agony.

"*Be still!*" the guard beside her roared.

The screams ceased, startling Isabeau into awareness. It occurred to her then that she had been the one screaming. The realisation brought on a fresh wave of heart-rending sobs. Nestled against her filthy brocade dress, her newborn son wailed along with her.

Struggling against the guards that held her, she craned her neck to catch a glimpse of her husband—but he was gone.

During the two years of their imprisonment together, they had strengthened one another. Now, just after the birth of their first child—the solace of their bondage—they had been torn apart. As the guards pried her from her husband, forcing them in opposite directions, her beloved had called, urgently, "Be strong and of a good courage, *ma chère*." She knew they were taking him to the galleys. She knew she would never see him again.

Oh, God! Isabeau sobbed. *Oh, God, where are you?*

Two guards manhandled her down a narrow hallway, out into the sunlight. A gust of cool wind rippled over her, drawing a shudder. "Where are you taking me?" she heard herself ask.

"I demand that you tell me."

The guard's grip on her arm tightened and his face hardened. "I don't answer to common criminals," he spat out.

Isabeau's eyes flashed. "I am not a criminal, Monsieur," she informed him icily. "I am the respected daughter of a noble French house, imprisoned for my faith."

He laughed, then jerked her forward until his face was inches away from hers. Isabeau gasped, clutching her small son closer.

"You are nothing more than a common criminal, imprisoned for defying the king's laws," he hissed menacingly. "And you will pay for your disobedience with your life."

The Tower of Constance, Aigues-Mortes, France March, 1737

Marie Durand was writing a letter when Mama Rouvier settled beside her, eyes alight. "Have you heard?" she whispered, her voice crackling.

Marie glanced up at her brother's mother-in-law, offering her a small smile. "Have you come to tell me the latest gossip?"

Mama Rouvier returned her smile. "They are sending a new prisoner today," she said. "I overheard the guards speaking when they let us out for our morning walk around the courtyard." She leaned close to whisper in Marie's ear. "It is a young noblewoman with a small child."

Marie raised her eyebrows. "Another child?"

Mama Rouvier nodded. "Apparently her husband was taken to the galleys."

Marie's heart clenched. She knew what it was like to be separated from someone she loved. Her mother and brother had been wrenched from her life when she was just eight years old. She had never seen her mother again. She had only seen her brother intermittently over the following decade before she was imprisoned herself. The pain was so devastating that she would not wish it on anyone. Marie tucked her letter beneath the flimsy pile of sheets that served as her bed, then stood.

"Come," she said, clasping Mama Rouvier's arm. "We need to prepare a place for her, right beside us."

When Isabeau arrived at the tower, she felt as though she had been dropped into the pit of hell, devoid of the attending flames. She gazed around the small circular room with wide-eyed terror. Dozens of pale, gaunt faces stared back, their sunken eyes taking her in with dull indifference.

Oh, God! she cried, swallowing back the bitter sting of tears. *Will I become like that?* For a moment, she couldn't breathe. She clutched her baby close, her eyes darting warily around the room, until they settled on a single smiling face. A young woman was approaching her from the far side of the room. She was as pale and gaunt as the rest of them, but there was something about her that drew Isabeau.

"I am Marie Durand," she said.

Isabeau gasped. "Durand?" she questioned. "Are you related to Pierre Durand?"

Marie nodded, a sad smile curving her lips. "I am his sister."

Isabeau reached out a hand to squeeze Marie's arm. "We were sorry to hear of his death."

Marie clasped Isabeau's hand. "And I was sorry to hear of your husband's plight."

Tears sprang to Isabeau's eyes, spilling over her lashes, trailing down her cheeks. "It has been so hard," she said, her voice cracking. "So hard."

Marie wrapped a thin arm around her shoulder, gently propelling her forward. "Come," she said softly. "We have prepared a place for you and the baby. It is not much, but at least you will not be alone."

Spring, 1742

"Couldn't they have sent us some brocade?" Isabeau asked, running her fingers over the coarse linen on her lap.

Marie merely snorted. She was taking inventory of the latest parcel of relief goods sent to them by Huguenots in exile. The governor had pitied the imprisoned women enough to forward the package, though his charity did not extend to setting them free. Marie had a letter listing all the items that had been sent, which she was carefully perusing as she inspected what lay before them. Around the room, women watched her in anticipation.

"A nice swathe of velvet or brocade would have made us all feel better," Isabeau insisted with a sniff. She had been suffering with a head cold for weeks. It had only been worsened by the rain that battered the tower, forcing them to lie shivering on wet bedding through the night.

"At least they sent some toys for Gallièn," Marie pointed out, glancing up in search of Isabeau's small son. He was five years old now—emaciated and sickly, but the light of Isabeau's life. Especially since she had received word of her husband's death.

"He's gone down to the courtyard with Mama Rouvier," Isabeau said when she noticed Marie looking for him.

Marie nodded.

"They sent so much rice," Isabeau muttered, sifting through the sack with dirty fingers. She sighed, closing her eyes. "Sometimes when I close my eyes, I can smell the bread and stew from the kitchens at our chateau."

"Tell me again what life was like at your grand chateau," Marie urged, going back to her inventory. Talking about her life before being imprisoned relieved Isabeau's distress.

Isabeau began to speak, describing the grounds, the house, the luxurious beds. "And baths whenever I wanted," she finished dreamily, "scented with dried orange peel from Spain." She pursed her lips, as her eyes fluttered open.

"Do you regret attending that secret worship service?" Marie asked softly. She had asked that question a thousand times in the past five years. She found repeating it reminded Isabeau not only of her choices but also of the convictions behind them. Speaking those convictions aloud strengthened Isabeau's flagging resolve.

"No, I do not regret my choices," Isabeau said softly. "I only regret getting caught." She shook her head. "No, that's not true. I regret the king's decision to make us outlaws simply because we choose to abide by Scripture and believe in salvation by faith. No-one deserves that."

Marie was just opening her mouth to agree when the large door to the prison cell creaked open. Gallièn rushed in, followed by a limping Mama Rouvier.

"Mama! Mama!" he cried, rushing to wrap his arms around Isabeau's neck. She laughed, gathering him close as she pressed kisses onto his cool cheeks.

"Did you have a good walk with Grand-Mère Rouvier?" she asked, cuddling him closer. He squirmed, pushing away from her to gaze up into her eyes.

"They have brought a new prisoner," he said with wide-eyed solemnity.

Marie's gaze flew to Mama Rouvier, who was lowering herself to her small pallet.

Nodding, she rubbed her back. "A young woman, about the same age as you both," she said, leaning back against the cold stone wall with a groan.

Marie and Isabeau glanced at each other. "She has a child," Mama Rouvier continued. "An infant."

Immediately, the two young women sprang into action. Isabeau sorted through her bedding, setting aside a few sheets and quilts to make a new pallet, while Marie rummaged through the newly arrived supplies in search of more cloth. They had just assembled a few necessities when the door creaked open, disgorging a young woman into their midst. She clutched a wailing infant to her breast, and as she took in her dreary, filthy surroundings, she crumpled to the floor sobbing. Isabeau and Marie rushed over to her.

"*Shhh, ma chère*," Isabeau murmured, running a gentle hand over her head. "All will be well." Her words only caused the young woman to cry harder.

Marie put an arm around her shoulders. "Come," she said, urging the young woman to stand. "Let us get you settled."

When she raised her tear-stained face, Marie smiled. "What is your name?" she asked softly.

The young woman sniffed. "Anne," she replied. "Anne Goutez."

Marie squeezed her close. "Well, Anne, you may be cast down, but I guarantee you are not forsaken or alone."

Spring, 1745

Sometimes friendship is the only barrier that stands between us and despair. Isabeau knew this to be true. She lay on her side, curled into a ball, rocking herself in the dim light of breaking day. She had been unable to sleep yet again. The straw beneath her was damp, her head pounded, and she felt feverish. Yet, none of those things was responsible for keeping her awake. Beside her, she felt Marie stir, then reach over to place a comforting hand on her arm.

"Do you want to pray?" she whispered, squeezing Isabeau's shoulder.

"I have no words left," Isabeau replied despondently. Nor did she have tears or strength or the will to live. But day by day, she forced herself to go on because of the three women in her life who had become more than family. Marie began to pray beside her, pleading with God for comfort. Isabeau squeezed her eyes shut, feeling the salty sting of tears spilling over her cheeks.

Nearly a year ago, guards had entered their chamber to take Gallièn away from her. She had screamed, lunging at them in desperation, but they had knocked her back, wrangling her wailing son through the door. He was six—the age that the state took possession of children whose parents were Protestant heretics. He would be placed in a home somewhere, or perhaps a monastery, where he would be raised Catholic. She would never see him again.

In the days and weeks that followed, she pleaded with God to take her life, but she still lived. Marie forced her to eat. Their new friend Anne took her outdoors to walk every day. Isabeau found some consolation in tending Anne's small daughter, but the experience was always bittersweet as she thought of Gallièn at that age.

A clear voice began to sing a psalm, achingly sweet. It was Anne. She grasped Isabeau's hand, rubbing her thumb over the parchment-thin skin, while she filled the air with the comfort of scripture.

Later, when they had returned from their morning walk, Isabeau was feeling somewhat better until a guard came through the door, grimly informing them of the intendant's imminent arrival.

The women huddled together in groups. "He's coming to offer recantations," Marie said, certainty infusing her voice.

"He is wasting his time," Mama Rouvier muttered, watching Anne's daughter play.

Anne bit her lip. "If I recant, I will be able to leave this place and take Jeanne with me," she whispered. "I won't have to . . ." she paused, glancing at Isabeau before falling silent.

"You won't have to face losing your child," Marie finished for her.

Isabeau sucked in a breath. She thought back on the times when she, too, had been offered the opportunity to recant. She had refused every overture. Her conscience was not for sale, she had told them. They could imprison her in a tower, but they could never take away her freedom. Some of the other women had urged her to consider it for Gallièn's sake.

"Think of your son," one of them had said. "If you leave, you can keep him. If you stay, they will take him as soon as he turns six."

"If I recant, what kind of example will I set for him?" Isabeau had countered. "I want to show him that his conscience cannot be bought."

That had settled the matter. She had not anticipated the full agony of losing her son, but she could not regret the choice she had made to remain true to her faith. It was what her husband would have wanted.

"What will you do?" Marie asked Anne quietly.

Anne shook her head. "I don't know." She buried her face in her hands with a sob. "Why are they so cruel? Why will they not allow us to worship God according to our conscience? We have hurt no-one. We are good citizens, yet they treat us like criminals." She turned to Isabeau, eyes wild and pleading. "If you could choose again, if you could spare yourself the agony of losing Gallièn, would you recant?"

Isabeau laid a gentle hand against her cheek. "I would not, *chère*," she said softly, "but I am not you. You must make your own choice—between you and God."

Burying her face in her hands, Anne sobbed. "I can't," she wailed. "Oh, God, I do not have the strength to choose!"

"Then let us ask God to strengthen you," Marie said softly.

Isabeau and Marie placed their arms around Anne and began to pray.

When it was Anne's turn to face Monsieur Lenain, the king's intendant, she felt faint. She stood before him as his gaze raked over her, then his eyes dropped down to the sheet of parchment before him. He read it quickly, then pushed it across the table towards her, holding out a quill.

"Sign here, then go down to the village, attend a single mass and you will be released today." His gaze flicked over her face. "You and your little daughter."

Anne sucked in a breath but remained motionless.

"Well?" he demanded, waving the quill before her impatiently. "What are you waiting for?"

"I will not recant," she said quietly, her voice scratchy from hours of crying.

His eyes widened in disbelief. "Were you not present when they came to take away Madame Menet's son several months ago?"

Anne nodded. Yes, she had been there. She had held Isabeau as she wept, kept watch beside her night after night, praying and singing. She had walked the path of suffering beside her sister and friend. She would not wish such agony on anyone, least of all herself.

"And yet you hesitate to recant?" Lenain asked.

"I will not be bought, monsieur," Anne replied. "My conscience is devoted to God and His Word."

Lenain barked out a humourless laugh, then leaned back against his chair. "That is a pretty phrase, Madame, but your conscience will not save your child. Nor will it save you."

"You cannot have it!" she shouted, losing her grip on her roiling emotions. "You can treat us like animals, you can strip us of every earthly comfort, but you cannot touch our faith, our conscience, our will. All those belong to God alone!"

Lenain watched her, measuring her with his steely eyes. "Your God cannot save you," he finally said with a sneer.

"My God is well able to save me," Anne said with quiet certainty, her mind snapping to the words of the three Hebrew boys as they stood before another tyrant. "But even if he does not, I will not bow down to you."

Lenain's gaze hardened, his lips pinching together. He rose slowly from his chair, leaning menacingly over the table before him.

"I own your destiny, madame," he said icily. "You would do well to remember that."

"You do not own me, monsieur," Anne spat out. "You only think you do."

For a moment, she thought he might strike her. Instead, he snatched up the parchment before him and ripped it to shreds.

Tossing the fragments into the air, he smirked at her. "You will die in this place."

Anne narrowed her eyes. "That is for God to decide, monsieur, not you."

When they led Anne back to the prison chamber, she noticed the room was emptier. Isabeau, Marie and Mama Rouvier were all huddled in a corner while Jeanne slept soundly on her pallet. There were four other women on the far side of the room. Eight of them in total. When they had woken up that morning, there had been more than 30.

Marie smiled when she saw Anne. Rising, she held out her arms and Anne fell into them sobbing.

"All will be well, *ma chère*," Marie whispered, rocking her gently.

Anne felt Isabeau's arms wrap around her as well, felt the dampness of her tears against her temple.

"God sees," Isabeau whispered, "and God knows."

They stood clutching each other as they wept—sisters of faith, love and hope.

Marie Durand was born in 1711. Her parents Etienne and Claudine Durand chose to remain in France after the Revocation of the Edict of Nantes, which robbed French Protestants of their civil and religious liberty. Her mother was arrested during a raid on a Huguenot worship service when she was only eight years old. Her brother, Pierre, was ordained in 1724, despite a law forbidding the ordination of Protestant ministers. Marie was arrested and taken to the Tower of Constance at the age of 19, in 1730. Her crime was twofold—she was the sister of a Protestant minister and a heretic herself. Despite repeated attempts to secure her recantation, Marie refused, persisting in maintaining both her faith and her religious liberty. She was imprisoned for 38 years before finally being released in April, 1768.

A Bond That Strengthens

Isabeau Menet was a noble woman who lost everything when she and her husband were arrested during a raid on a Huguenot worship service in Beauchastel, in the Vivarais. She was imprisoned for two years before she and her husband were separated. He was sent to the galleys where he died, and she was sent to the Tower of Constance. She gave birth to her son while imprisoned in Pont-Saint-Esprit, shortly before she was transferred to the Tower of Constance. She lost her husband and her son, yet stood firm against repeated attempts to force her recantation. Unfortunately, Isabeau later had a nervous breakdown. In 1750, she was released from prison and returned to her family, having been deemed insane.

Little is known of Anne Goutez except that she, too, was arrested during a raid on a Huguenot worship service. Her husband was sent to the galleys, while she and her infant daughter were sent to the Tower of Constance. Her husband died shortly after his arrest; Anne prevailed. She was released from prison just before Marie Durand, sometime in 1767.

These women provide an example of the power of friendship to help others remain faithful—even at extreme cost.

19

Elizabeth of Denmark

A Faithful Witness

Spandau Castle, Berlin, Germany
Easter, 1527

Being caught red-handed is a nasty business, especially when you're discovered by your own child.

Elizabeth watched the scene unfold, numb with shock. She noted—with detached horror—that the slender, hooded figure that had barged through the door of her presence chamber was not a young groom, as she had first thought, but her own newlywed daughter, home for a visit at Easter. She saw Elsa's face pale as she realised what was going on, the outrage that pinched her features as her gaze tripped over the occupants of the chamber before landing on her mother's face.

"What are you doing?" she demanded, her shrill voice edging towards hysteria.

Elizabeth was caught between tears and laughter. She had planned this all so carefully—organised the reformist minister, made sure her family would be out hunting, paid off the servants to keep them silent, arranged the rooms to the minister's specifications. She had done everything with an eye to detail, and now—

"Is Father aware of what you're up to?" Elsa asked, hysteria now edged out by a more terrifying icy calm.

Elizabeth remained immobile, watching her child.

"If you will not answer me, then perhaps you will answer him," Elsa ground out as the silence lengthened.

Her words drew a gasp from the frazzled minister. His hand began to tremble, causing the cup he held to tip precariously. He had been about to end the communion service. It had been lovely. Refreshing. Elizabeth had revelled in this new way of expressing her faith in Christ—her first communion as a follower of the way of salvation by faith. It had been everything she had hoped for, until her daughter had burst into the room and ruined everything.

"There's no need for threats," Elizabeth said, rising from her chair with practised aplomb. She was the Electress of Brandenburg, a royal Danish princess. She would not allow this railing scrap of humanity she had birthed to intimidate her, regardless of how perilous her position was.

"How could you!" Elsa continued to rant, her agitation growing with each passing moment.

The reformist minister, who had been interrupted during his closing prayer, was now fumbling to gather up his belongings, desperately shoving things into receptacles. It would have been funny had it not been so awful. Elizabeth cast a glance at one of her ladies and the woman immediately sprang into action. They had planned for all contingencies, including the very real threat of discovery. Their first order of business was to ensure the minister got away safely before her husband discovered his presence within the castle. Elizabeth discreetly moved forward to conceal the activity behind her while confronting her belligerent daughter.

"Elsa—" she began, raising her hands placatingly.

However, Elsa had a mind of her own. She shot her mother a final mutinous glare before striding from the room. "You will regret this, Mother!" she shouted over her shoulder.

Elizabeth's blood turned to ice. Her husband hated reformists. He had been one of Luther's most outspoken opponents at the Diet of Worms. He had been one of the first German princes to enforce the Edict of Worms calling for Luther's arrest. He had worked tirelessly to ensure his realms remained free of the Lutheran heresy. And now his daughter was about to tell him that a heretic lived right beneath his nose—in his own house.

November, 1527

Elizabeth disliked bargaining, but she had been forced to negotiate terms in the aftermath of the debacle at Easter. Elsa had gone straight to her father who had confronted Elizabeth in a rage, insisting that she immediately recant her faith. Instead of capitulating, she had pleaded for time. She reasoned that she needed time to rethink her position. She argued that she could not be expected to yield to coercion and asked for a six-month reprieve.

Joachim shrewdly agreed to her terms because he knew he couldn't force her will. He also knew that she had nowhere else to go. He believed her helpless condition would eventually produce willing submission. Elizabeth had tried desperately over the past six months to formulate a plan of escape. Nothing had worked. Her brother, the King of Denmark, was languishing in exile. And while her uncle, the Elector of Saxony, was willing to have her, Joachim watched her like a hawk, encircling her with a network of spies. It was impossible to do anything without his knowledge.

Now her time was up. She was seated in the chapel at Spandau Castle watching the Romanist priest prepare to administer the mass.

"You will bow to the host and partake of the mass in the orthodox manner," Joachim hissed beside her. "And you will renew your allegiance to the true church and cease this dithering with Luther and his heresy."

Elizabeth had never seen her husband so angry. Then again, she had never before done anything so blatantly opposed to his will in all their years of marriage. Elizabeth supposed it would be easy to just comply and be done with it, but she thought of all the other brave reformists who had gone before her—Luther at Worms featuring most prominently in her mind—and she simply couldn't bring herself to bow and scrape while she relinquished her freedom. She could not recant. She would not. She gritted her teeth, choosing to remain silent.

Her husband had summoned all their children and their spouses to watch her humiliation. He wanted to make sure everyone knew she was sincere in her repentance. What he had not bargained for was the possibility that she might refuse to obey him.

When the priest began his invocation, Joachim turned to face her. "Now, Elizabeth," he hissed.

She raised her chin and shook her head.

He leaped to his feet. "You will recant, or I will see you thrown in the dungeon for your defiance!" His loud voice startled the priest and elicited gasps from their daughters, who sat behind them.

Elizabeth felt the sting of tears but refused to surrender to them. She would not cry. She would not allow any of them to see how deeply this treatment bruised her spirit.

"Elizabeth!" Joachim thundered. "You will bow! Now!"

Drawing in a breath, she steeled herself before meeting his eyes. "I will not," she said quietly.

"And so you will be one of these vile Lutherans?" he shouted. "You will blaspheme the Holy Church and her sacraments while you turn my castle into a seminary of heresy?" He paced away from her, trembling with rage. "I won't have it, Elizabeth! Do you hear me? I will not have it! It is your duty to obey me as your husband and to honour the Holy Roman Church."

"I must obey God rather than man," Elizabeth countered, keeping her voice steady and even.

"I am your husband!" Joachim shouted.

"Yes," Elizabeth agreed, shocked by how reasonable she sounded. "But you are not my God."

Joachim whirled on her, his hands balled into fists, his face red with rage. Elizabeth was certain he would strike her. It was at this juncture that her sons-in-law intervened, rushing forward, pleading with her husband to calm himself and offering the suggestion that Elizabeth be granted another six months to consider her actions.

She glanced over her shoulder at her children, who sat stone-faced, refusing to meet her gaze. She was bitterly disappointed that none of them had come to her defence. She knew they dared not defy their father, she knew that they were staunch Romanists, yet she had hoped that they would at least plead with him on her behalf.

Finally, Joachim corralled his temper, agreeing to grant her an extension of six more months. When Elizabeth was escorted back to her chambers by her palace guards, she knew she had arrived at a crossroads. Joachim would not grant her another reprieve. If she wanted to retain her faith, if she wanted to survive, then she needed to escape.

March, 1528

The opportune moment for liberation arrived unexpectedly, but Elizabeth was prepared. Her husband went to visit their daughter Elsa and her husband in Braunschweig one day in March, and that very night Elizabeth set her plans in motion. She had carefully crafted her escape, enlisting the aid of her uncle, the Elector of Saxony, and her brother, the King of Denmark.

"Is everything ready?" she asked Götse, the gatekeeper at the castle who had sworn his loyalty to her.

"Yes, Your Grace," he whispered, his eyes darting about the deserted courtyard.

They hurried across the cobbled expanse on silent feet, Elizabeth dressed like a peasant, accompanied by a single trusted maid. Götse opened a small door set into the wall beside the massive portcullis and Elizabeth ducked her head to creep through. She slid down the steep embankment to the waiting boat bobbing in the castle's moat.

The night was partially lit by a waning moon, but the shadows were deep enough to hide them. When they were safely inside the rickety craft, the boatman took up the oars. Elizabeth cringed with every creak and splash that murmured through the still night, sure that one of her husband's guards would discover them making their escape. They disembarked the small boat on the far shore of the moat, then hurried to a waiting wagon, which conveyed them down rutted roads towards the electoral castle in Torgau.

When the wagon clattered through the gates of the castle, Elizabeth felt her tenuous hold on her emotions begin to crack. The waiting grooms helped her alight, then a servant guided her through the winding stone hallways of the castle to her uncle's presence chamber. When her uncle saw her, he strode forward to greet her. His face, filled with tender concern, snapped the final thread of Elizabeth's composure. Her knees gave way beneath her and she sank to the cold floor sobbing, overwhelmed by the weight of what she had done.

Her uncle knelt before her, placing a comforting hand on her shoulder. "All will be well, my dear," he murmured gently. "All will be well."

But Elizabeth couldn't fathom how anything in her life would ever be well again.

Lichtenburg Castle, Saxony, Germany
July, 1535

When the messenger came to tell her Joachim was dead, Elizabeth wept. She remembered the husband of her youth who had adored her, the first happy years of their marriage when they had been certain nothing could disturb their joy. Then her mind alighted on the final painful years leading to this moment of grief. She relived Joachim's rage when he found out she had left him, the ensuing legal battles, his refusal to support her financially, the bitter sting of poverty and privation. Through it all, her greatest consolation was seeing her beloved Elsa—the child who had betrayed her—embrace the Reformation wholeheartedly. When she saw Elsa set free by the truth of salvation by faith, Elizabeth realised that there truly was no greater joy than to see her children walk in truth.

Her oldest son, Joachim, came to her soon after her husband's death. She had known he would come. She also knew what he would ask of her.

"It's time to come home, Mother," he said quietly.

"Where is home?" she wanted to know. Seven years of battling her husband and moving from place to place had stripped her of her roots.

"Spandau," Joachim said without hesitation. "I know you love the place, and I know Father . . . I know the castle was a wedding gift."

"Your father was a good man," Elizabeth said, a sad smile flickering across her face. "He was simply misguided." She studied her son's face. "Tell me, Achim," she said, "if I come home to Spandau, will you allow me the freedom to worship according to my conscience? Will you allow my household and the tenants on my estates to embrace the Reformation? Will you allow me to conduct church services as I see fit, with a Lutheran minister?"

His resigned sigh told her everything she needed to know. He stood up, paced to the small window, then pivoted to face her.

"On his death bed," he began, "Father made me promise him that I would not allow Brandenburg to become Lutheran. He made me promise that when I became elector, I would not allow Luther's heresy to infiltrate the realm."

Elizabeth shook her head in disbelief. *The nerve of the man!* Even on his deathbed he was dictating terms to her, looking for ways to thwart her. He would have known that when he was gone Achim would approach Elizabeth with an offer to return home.

"I can't defy his wishes, Mother."

"Yet you will disregard mine," Elizabeth stated, bitterness creeping into her voice.

"I cannot please you both!" Achim exclaimed, exasperated. "God knows I have tried these past seven years, though I have never managed to accomplish it."

Elizabeth softened. "You don't have to please me, Son," she said. "Neither do you have to please your father. Not at the expense of pleasing God."

Summer, 1545

The stalemate between Elizabeth and Achim dragged on for a decade. He sent his mother money, determined that she should live as comfortably as a dowager electress ought. She prayed for him constantly, determined that this child of hers should embrace the truth that had so deeply touched her heart. He continued to ask her to come home. She continued to ask him if he would allow her to preach the Word of God within the boundaries of her estates.

Then one day, she was told that her son had come to visit her. When Elizabeth swept into the room to greet him, Achim's face broke into a wide smile.

"What is it?" she asked, staring at him in bewilderment.

He was always morose when he came to see her, acting like he had when he was a small boy and she refused to give him some treat or trinket he had asked for. But today he was not petulant or pouty, he was jubilant. Immediately, her suspicions were aroused.

"What has happened?" Elizabeth repeated, approaching her son with caution.

"I've come to bring you home," he said.

"And are you—" Elizabeth began, but Achim cut her off.

"I've accepted the gospel, Mother," he blurted out. "I believe as you do, and I would like nothing better than for you to come home and preach the gospel to as many people as you please."

Elizabeth gaped at him, her eyes welling with unexpected tears. "What?" she whispered. "How?"

"It is a long story," he said, coming forward to clasp her hands. "But suffice it to say that God answered my mother's prayers and brought her stubborn son into the light."

Elizabeth raised a trembling hand and cupped his cheek—not the cheek of the little boy she had once rocked to sleep but the cheek of a grown man who had mustered the courage to please his heavenly Father at the expense of pleasing his earthly one.

"Well, then," she said, as tears spilled down her cheeks, "I suppose it's time I finally came home."

Elizabeth of Denmark, Electress of Brandenburg, was born in 1485 to King John of Denmark and Christina of Saxony. About 25 years after her marriage to Joachim I, Elector of Brandenburg, Elizabeth embraced the ideas of the Reformation—most likely through her brother, Christian II of Denmark, who was exposed to Luther's teachings during a period of exile in Saxony. Elizabeth's acceptance of the Reformation destroyed her once-happy marriage and alienated her from her children. She spent nearly 18 years in exile in Saxony. During this time, Elizabeth's position made her a public witness for her faith in a way that was unique for the time. Through her influence and prayers, four of her children eventually accepted the Protestant faith, and on her return to Spandau Castle, she preached the gospel to her household, tenants and anyone else willing to hear. On her death bed, she requested that she be buried beside her husband, despite the acrimonious breakdown of their marriage nearly 30 years before.

20

Katharina Zell

A CIRCLE OF REFUGE

Kensingen, Duchy of Austria
Summer, 1524

Jakob Otter had always known his mouth would get him into trouble, but he hadn't imagined the magnitude or depth of it. He was a stranger here, having come to minister in the little town of Kensingen with high hopes of seeing it embrace reform. He had been exceedingly gratified when it had. But then the mayor had been hauled off to jail for his new faith, and the town clerk had been tried for heresy. And it was all his doing.

"I will leave," Jakob said, as he watched the clerk being led to the gallows. His words were decisive, but he looked to the friend beside him, seeking confirmation his decision was a wise one.

The man nodded his agreement reluctantly. "The church here needs you," he said with a heavy sigh. "Heaven knows, I believe you speak the truth, but it doesn't matter what I think. I am nothing more than a lowly caretaker employed by His Grace."

Wolf von Hürnheim was hardly a lowly caretaker. He had been given the mortgage of Kensingen by Archduke Ferdinand, which meant he owned the town and was responsible for its operation. In theory, he could do whatever he wanted with it, but the reality was that if Wolf so much as breathed incorrectly, the archduke would fall on him with all the military might of Austria.

Jakob weighed his options again in silence. He didn't want to leave his flock. He felt compelled to care for them, to preach the gospel. What kind of shepherd would he be if he left them? Yet, he did not want to die. Nor did he want more of his congregation to suffer.

Watching the clerk stand beneath the shadow of the noose, he knew it should have been him facing the scaffold. He also knew why it was not. Peasants in the surrounding regions were already revolting right and left. If the archduke martyred Jakob, it was almost certain the people of Kensingen would revolt at the loss of their beloved minister. The archduke couldn't afford to take such a risk unless he was provoked beyond endurance. Strangling the clerk was an act of aggression—a warning.

"No-one wants to see you dead, Jakob," Wolf continued, "least of all me. But I must do what I am told, and if you won't stop preaching—" He held up a hand as Jakob began to protest. "And I know you can't—then you need to leave. For all our sakes."

They watched as the hangman wound the noose around the clerk's slender neck. The man cried out, pleading with God to have mercy upon his soul. The crowd murmured, some among them casting surreptitious glances at Jakob, while others moaned, covering their eyes.

When the hangman kicked aside the small stool the clerk stood upon, Jakob averted his gaze. He heard the snap and creak of the noose, a gasp from the crowd, followed by a prolonged moment of silence. Jakob felt his surroundings dip and sway. Wolf's arm shot out to steady him. Groaning, he buried his face in his hands as the realisation washed over him—he had exhausted all his options.

Jakob had thought he could slip out of Kensingen unnoticed. After all, it was a weekday and most citizens were going about their business. But as he neared the city gates, his eyes widened. He ground to a halt, gaping at the spectacle before him.

A crowd of women stood before him, barring his way to the city gate. He had never seen so many of them congregated together before. When they saw him, they bobbed towards him like a gaggle of geese in their starched white caps and aprons. They looked mildly angry.

Good heavens! he thought, his mind swirling in panic. *Is this how the archduke means to kill me? Has he sent a group of women to do me in?* He knew, even as he thought it, that this was a preposterous idea, but he couldn't fathom the reason for their presence.

"We won't let you leave!" one of the women shouted, moving to stand at the helm of the group.

Jakob's eyes grew larger. "What?" he sputtered.

"We're not going to let you leave," she repeated, and everyone murmured their assent.

Then Jakob noticed a few men in the crowd—cobblers, tailors, butchers and bakers. They were men he often did business with, men who were his parishioners. He began to recognise the women as well. All of them belonged to his congregation.

"I *must* go," he said weakly. Then he cleared his throat and added, "If I do not, they will send me the way of the town clerk. Is that what you want?" It was a feeble attempt at gaining sympathy, but Jakob suddenly felt desperate. If they formed a mob to force him to stay, the archduke was sure to kill him for being a troublemaker. He could ill afford a peasant revolt instigated by members of his flock in a misguided attempt to prevent his leave-taking.

"No, Herr Otter!" one of the women shouted. "You are going to stay and preach to us."

Jakob shook his head and took a step backwards, holding up his hands, but it was no use. They advanced on him, laid their hands upon him and jostled him down the street to the church, swearing by imperial law that they would protect him. He was too dumbfounded at being accosted by a group of female citizens to put up much of a fight. When they arrived at the church, he mounted the pulpit and obliged them with a sermon.

All was well until Wolf arrived with a contingent of guards, and Jakob knew his time had run out.

The Free Imperial City of Strasbourg, Germany Summer, 1524

Nothing flustered Katharina Zell. She was a stalwart woman who was too practical to be jarred by the unexpected. Nor was she afraid to swim upstream. If she had been, she would not have married her husband—a Catholic priest turned reformer intent on proving the absurdity of celibacy by taking a wife. Katharina Zell had nerves of steel. Or so she had thought until a large group of fleeing men shook her self-confidence.

Her husband, Matthew, stood before her, flushed and agitated, while she gaped at him, wide-eyed. "*How* many?" she asked.

"One hundred and fifty," he replied.

"Where on earth have they come from?" she asked, glancing around their small parsonage and mentally calculating how much food she had in her larder.

Matthew motioned for her to follow him before striding towards the door.

"Matthew, wait!" she called, hurrying after him. "Who are they? And where have they come from?"

Matthew carried on, calling over his shoulder, "They are from Kensingen."

Katharina quickened her pace to keep up with him. Ahead of them, near the cathedral, she spied a growing crowd of people. "Kensingen in Austria?" she questioned.

Matthew nodded, slowing his stride a fraction. "They are seeking refuge here."

Katharina wasn't completely surprised by this. After all, she and Matthew had hosted countless refugees fleeing religious persecution. But 150 of them all at once?

"Who will care for them all?" she asked.

Matthew met her eyes, telling her everything she needed to know. She was now the proud beneficiary of 150 refugees from Kensingen. Firming her resolve, she marched forward.

As Katharina listened to the men of Kensingen telling their tale, she found that the group was guarding one reformist minister—Jakob Otter. They claimed that Otter had been exiled from Kensingen for spreading reformist ideas. Their overlord, Wolf von Hürnheim, had personally asked him to leave.

"But our wives wouldn't hear of it," one of the men said.

Katharina shook her head in wonder. "So, you're saying all your wives," she paused, contemplating the crowd packed into a corner of the cathedral, "—all your wives stood before Herr Otter and refused to let him leave Kensingen?"

Jakob nodded, perspiration lining his brow. He was a small man, slender and pale, almost fragile in appearance.

Katharina wasn't surprised that he needed 150 men to protect him, but she was surprised by the boldness of the women of Kensingen. Not only had they tried to prevent his flight, but when he had been forced to flee, the women had insisted their husbands accompany the minister for his protection. Seeing no reason to deny their request, Wolf von Hürnheim had agreed, though the Archduke Ferdinand now considered the men traitors and exiled. The husbands of Kensingen had meekly acquiesced to their wives' demands and the entire company—with Jakob Otter at its centre—had travelled down to the Rhine and boarded a ship to Strasbourg.

"We knew," one of the men said, "that Herr Zell would not turn us away."

Katharina eyed him. *Herr Zell indeed!* she thought in exasperation, but then she drew in a deep breath.

"You are right," she said with a brisk nod. "Herr Zell will not turn you away."

There was a collective exhalation of breath as relief washed over the men like a tidal wave. But Katharina felt a sudden determination.

"Right," she barked, like a general marshalling her troops to war. "Seventy of you will board with us and the rest of you will be billeted to homes in the city. I will see to your meals." She drew in a deep breath, nodded once more and clapped her hands. "Come on then, let's be on our way."

Kensingen, Duchy of Austria
July, 1524

Meanwhile, in far off Kensingen, 150 women were hard at work keeping their farms afloat and their children fed. None of them regretted sacrificing the presence of their husbands, for they knew they had done what was right, good and necessary. Herr Otter had been a stranger in their midst, arriving unexpectedly in their city and blessing them with the good news. Protecting him was their Christian duty. Yet there were times when weariness overtook them, and loneliness wrapped around them like a shroud. It was during one of these seasons that they received a letter—a rather long letter— from Strasbourg.

"Who is it from?" someone wondered.

"The wife of Matthew Zell," read another, holding the letter in her chapped hands.

There were gasps and murmurs among the group, as each wondered why Mistress Zell was writing to them.

"Read it aloud!" someone shouted.

The woman who held it in her hands nodded, laid the crinkled sheets on her lap, smoothed them out and began to read:

> To my fellow sisters in Christ,
>
> Day and night I pray God that He may increase your faith that you forget not His invincible Word. Remember the word of the Lord to the

A Circle of Refuge

prophet Isaiah: "Can a woman forget her sucking child? . . . They may forget, yet I will not forget thee." Are these not golden words? Faith is not faith which is not tried . . .

As the lone voice continued to read, a hush fell over the gathered crowd. They had sent away their men, worked tirelessly to protect their minister and daily faced the threat of renewed persecution. How comforting it was to know amid it all that someone they barely knew was thinking of them and praying for them.

Nothing is known about the brave women of Kensingen beyond what has been related in this story. Their husbands returned in September, 1524, after the Archduke Ferdinand pardoned them.

Katharina Zell (neé Schütz) was born around 1497 in the Free Imperial City of Strasbourg. She heard of Martin Luther's teachings when Matthew Zell arrived at the Cathedral of Strasbourg as parish priest. They were married in 1524, and their two children died in infancy. Katharina was a tireless advocate for various social causes—championing the care of Protestant refugees, caring for students and guests, and helping the poor. She cared for the needs of the Kensingen refugees for nearly two months. Katharina was also a prolific writer, championing the gospel as ferociously as she championed her other causes. She hosted Calvin, remonstrated with Luther, spent time with Melanchthon and visited the fanatical Anabaptist Melchior Hoffman in prison. She died in 1562, an advocate of Scripture and service to the end.

Acknowledgments

Sometimes writing a book can be like running a marathon, and getting to the finish line requires a small village of people supporting your journey.

This book would not have been possible without my brilliant editor, Lauren Webb. Thank you for your patience, input, encouragement and support.

Thanks to Nathan Brown, Andrew Irvine and the team at Signs Publishing for giving me the opportunity to release yet another book baby into the wild. Your support has been a tremendous blessing.

Thanks to my family for their continued love and support. Nena, especially, for brainstorming, listening to me rant and offering invaluable input.

My husband Asela—for your unfailing support, in everything, always.

My girls, Elyse and Carys, my sternest critics, my fiercest supporters and the inspiration behind my work. I thank my God upon every remembrance of you.

Last but not least, thank you to my readers—so many of you have reached out to me over the years, offering your encouragement and support. You have been a blessing to me on this journey, and I pray that this book will draw you closer to Jesus.

Bibliography

Anderson, J (1857/58), *Ladies of the Reformation*, Blackie and Son, London.

Bainton, RH (1974), *Women of the Reformation in Germany and Italy*, Augsburg Publishing House, Minneapolis.

Bainton, RH (1977), *Women of the Reformation From Spain to Scandinavia*, Augsburg Publishing House, Minneapolis.

Beilin, EV (Ed.) (1996), *The Examinations of Anne Askew*, Oxford University Press, USA.

Bryson, A (1999), "Letter from Jeanne de Albert to Nicholas de Flotard, Viscount Gourdon, August 1555," in *Queen Jeanne and the Promised Land*, Brill, Leiden.

Campi, E (2004), "Heinrich Bullinger the theologian," *Annex: Magazine of the Reformierte Presse*, 3–12.

Cholakian, PF (2006), *Marguerite de Navarre: Mother of the Renaissance*, Columbia University Press, New York.

Derksen, J (1997), "Hans Adam and Jörg Ziegler: Strasbourg's radical tailors," *The Journal of Mennonite Studies*, 15, 31–43.

Derksen, J (2004), "Nonviolent political action in sixteenth-century Strasbourg: the Ziegler brothers," *Mennonite Quarterly Review*, 78(4), 543–556.

Felch, SM (Ed.) (2008), *The Morning and Evening Prayers of Elizabeth Tyrwhit*, Aldsgate Publishing, London.

Markham, CBD (2022), "Marie Durand: French Protestant prisoner and letter writer," PhD thesis, University of Western Australia.

Pipkin, AC (2022), *Dissenting Daughters: Reformed Women in the Dutch Republic 1572–1725*, Oxford University Press, Oxford.

Porter, L (2010), *Katherine the Queen: the Remarkable Life of Katherine Parr*, Macmillan, London.

Reid, JA (2009), *King's Sister – Queen of Dissent: Marguerite of Navarre (1492–1549) and Her Evangelical Network*, Brill, Boston.

Schneider-Böklen, E (2017), "Elizabeth Cruciger – nun, minister's wife and first Lutheran poetess," *Journal of the European Society of Women in Theological Research,* 25, 117–129.

Scott, T, Bagchi, AK (1979), "The Peasants' War: a historiographical review: part II," *The Historical Journal,* 22(4), 953–974, <https://doi.org/2638660>.

Scott, T (2011), "The collective response of women to early reforming preaching: four small communities and their preachers compared," *Archiv für Reformationsgeschichte,* 102(1), 7–32, <https://doi.org/10.14315/arg-2011-102-1-7>.

Snyder, CA, Huebert Hecht, LA (Eds) (1996), *Profiles of Anabaptist Women: Sixteenth Century Reforming Pioneers*, Canadian Corporation for Studies in Religion.

Stjerna, KI (Ed.) (2022), *Women Reformers of Early Modern Europe: Profiles, Texts, and Contexts*, Augsburg Fortress, <https://doi.org/10.2307/j.ctv29sfwq3>.

Tylor, C (1892), *The Camisards: A Sequel to the Huguenots of the Seventeenth Century,* Simpkin, Marshall, Hamilton, Kent and Company Limited, London.

VanDoodewaard, R (2017), *Reformation Women: Sixteenth Century Women Who Shaped Christianity's Rebirth*, Reformation Heritage Books, Grand Rapids.

Weir, A (2023), *Queens of the Age of Chivalry: England's Medieval Queens,* Ballantine Books, New York.

Wilson, D (2018), *The Heretic and The Queen: How Two Women Changed the Religion of England*, Lion Hudson, Oxford.

Sukeshinie Goonatilleke is a writer, speaker and trainer, who works on projects ranging from television scriptwriting for Christian media ministries to producing Bible study and Christian history resources. She is author of *Sisters in Arms: Courageous Women of the Reformaton* (Signs Publishing, 2020) and *As Bright as the Stars: Dauntless Disciples of the Reformation* (Signs Publishing, 2024).

When she isn't researching or writing, Sukeshine is homeschooling her children, actively involved in her local church, baking or curled up with a good book. She lives in Melbourne, Australia with her husband and two daughters.